W9-CGZ-359

SPECIAL MESSAGE TO READERS

This book is published under the auspices of

THE ULVERSCROFT FOUNDATION

(registered charity No. 264873 UK)

Established in 1972 to provide funds for research, diagnosis and treatment of eye diseases. Examples of contributions made are: —

A Children's Assessment Unit at Moorfield's Hospital, London.

•

Twin operating theatres at the Western Ophthalmic Hospital, London.

•

A Chair of Ophthalmology at the Royal Australian College of Ophthalmologists.

•

The Ulverscroft Children's Eye Unit at the Great Ormond Street Hospital For Sick Children, London.

You can help further the work of the Foundation by making a donation or leaving a legacy. Every contribution, no matter how small, is received with gratitude. Please write for details to:

**THE ULVERSCROFT FOUNDATION,
The Green, Bradgate Road, Anstey,
Leicester LE7 7FU, England.
Telephone: (0116) 236 4325**

In Australia write to:

**THE ULVERSCROFT FOUNDATION,
c/o The Royal Australian College of
Ophthalmologists,
27, Commonwealth Street, Sydney,
N.S.W. 2010.**

CAST A DARK SHADOW

Young Derry Lainey finds the unconscious man and takes him home to be cared for by his father, Doc Lainey. When the man regains consciousness, he has no idea who he is or what he is doing in the Copperstones area. When the cold-blooded killer Lorn Catlin and his gang arrive in town, Catlin claims that the stranger is his brother Avery, a vicious outlaw. But is he really Avery Catlin, or is his supposed brother intent on keeping the true past a deadly secret?

LP
Black
549

DAN BLACK

CAST
A DARK
SHADOW

Complete and Unabridged

LINFORD
Leicester

First published in Great Britain in 1996 by
Robert Hale Limited, London

First Linford Edition
published 1999
by arrangement with
Robert Hale Limited, London

The right of Dan Black to be identified
as the author of this work has been asserted
by him in accordance with the
Copyright, Design and Patents Act, 1988

Copyright © 1996 by Dan Black
All rights reserved

British Library CIP Data

Black, Dan
    Cast a dark shadow.—Large print ed.—
Linford western library
    1. Western stories
    2. Large type books
    I. Title
    823.9'14 [F]

    ISBN 0–7089–5562–2

Published by
F. A. Thorpe (Publishing) Ltd.
Anstey, Leicestershire

Set by Words & Graphics Ltd.
Anstey, Leicestershire
Printed and bound in Great Britain by
T. J. International Ltd., Padstow, Cornwall

This book is printed on acid-free paper

For Tooty

1

A fiery gold and rose sunset blazed across the Californian sky, shading the vastness in a warm, vibrant glow. The day was dying fast, but it was sure going out in a blaze of glory.

One man stood alone on the brow of a sage-covered hill overlooking the flat expanse of plain which stretched out as far as the eye could see towards an infinite misty horizon.

Standing there, his tall, leanly muscled stature cast a long, dark shadow across the land, which aptly reflected the darkness in his soul.

When a man has no past, he can never look back; cut adrift from whatever life he had before the present. Here was such a man, void of memory, gazing searchingly into the far horizon, feeling the need to see more than what had happened since yesterday.

In a day, he'd lived a lifetime.

Viewing the distant horizon, his mind rewound the events of the last twenty-four hours . . .

It began when he regained consciousness in the home of Doctor Evett Lainey.

'How're you feeling?' the doc asked, leaning over him with a concerned look on his scrubbed, world-weary, fifty-year-old face. A pocket watch and chain hung from his brown waistcoat which he wore over a freshly laundered, white, collarless shirt, giving the impression of a professional man who was both precise and pristine.

'Everything's kinda fuzzy,' he muttered, feeling groggy and weaker than a kitten. 'Where am I?'

'You're in my home, I'm Doc Lainey. My boy, Derry, found you lying unconscious near the river. We nearly took you for dead. You've got a humdinger of a bump on your skull, feller. Lucky you weren't killed.' There was genuine concern in the doc's voice.

Instinctively, he put a hand up to feel the bump, and audibly winced in pain at the touch. 'What happened?'

'We were hoping you'd tell us,' the doc replied.

Us? It was then that he noticed a young woman standing a few feet away from his bedside. His vision was still a mite hazy, but she was a vision in herself. Golden-red hair framed a delicately pretty face, and she wore a dress that reminded him of sunshine and which gave a sun-kissed glow to her face like holding a buttercup under your chin.

'Can you tell us what happened?' the doc reiterated, interrupting his patient's secretly appreciative study of the young woman. 'You bein' a newcomer to town, nobody we've asked seems to know anything about you.'

'I, eh . . . ' he strained to remember. 'I . . . '

'What's your name, feller?' the doc eased another question at him.

His name? Alarm bells sounded in

3

his head. What was his name? He couldn't remember!

'Can you remember where you're from?'

The anxious expression in his deep-set, rivergreen eyes was all the answer the doc needed to confirm his diagnosis.

'I suspected this might happen, Amber.' The doc voiced his concern to the young woman.

Pushing himself up into a sitting position, he demanded to know what was going on. A single linen sheet was all that covered his nakedness.

'Now just you relax there, feller.' The doc's tone was calm and steady, but it was Amber's hands on his bare shoulders directing him to lie back down that reassured him most. Up close, he could see her eyes were like two topaz gemstones and her lips, soft rubies. Altogether, in name and in appearance, Amber was a truly precious gem of a creature.

'Like I said,' the doc began to explain slowly, 'you were found unconscious near the river with a lump the size of a man's fist on your skull. You've been out cold for the best part of a day. I suspect you may have lost your memory — temporarily,' he hastened to add.

'My father is a well-respected physician in these parts. You're in good hands,' Amber assured him further.

He didn't doubt it, though it was her hands which were the best medicine.

It was strange, he thought, that amid the awful emptiness and worry, he still found it in him to admire this young lady. She had a fresh, clean scent, like newly washed linen, and flowery overtones which reminded him of rosewater.

'What is it?' Amber asked, seeing a flicker of realization on his hard but handsome face.

'Are you wearing rosewater?'

She looked at her father, then back at him. 'Why, yes.'

'So, I do remember something,' he beamed with relief.

5

'I'm afraid it ain't as simple as that,' Doc Lainey explained. 'You see, when a person loses their memory, they remember most of the basic things which are stored in their mind. Things like talking, riding a horse, what colour the sky is. What they don't remember is who they are, who other people are. It's kinda confusing, I know, but you'll soon understand what I'm gettin' at.'

'How long you reckon it'll take before I can remember who I am?'

The doc shrugged. 'Hard to say, but you're a strong and healthy feller, so there's a good chance it won't be too long. Likely, it'll come back piece by piece; little things will trigger parts of your memory, until one day, everything returns back the way it was.'

Although Doc Lainey had advised him to lie in bed and sleep awhile, a restlessness stirred inside him, urging him to get up and start remembering. He had a heap of questions that urgently needed answers, so he was glad when the doc's talkative young son, Derry, took it upon himself to fill in as many gaps as possible.

Amber had laundered his jeans and dark blue shirt, which he wore with boots and a long duster coat and low-crowned stetson. The clothes on his back were the only possessions he had. No gun, no holster, no horse, no money — and no identity whatsoever.

'They must have robbed ya, mister,' Derry calculated as they walked the length of the small town of Copperstone Creek together. The gangly fourteen year old had a mop of unruly ginger hair and world-curious hazel eyes set in a pleasant freckle-sprinkled face which was as scrubbed as his father's.

He gave the boy a quizzical look.

'Amber checked your clothing for something which would tell us who ya were, but your pockets were clean empty, which ain't like any man I knows. None of us have seen you around town before, but you must have been heading here, being so close to the river an' all. Question is, why were you coming to Copperstone?'

'And where was I coming from?' his deep, husky voice added ominously.

The boy shrugged blankly. 'Father says you sound like a feller he used to know, and he was from Montana.'

'Montana?' he tested out the word, but got no spark of recognition.

'How about Arizona? Texas? New Mexico? Nevada?' The boy was trying to be helpful, but it wasn't having any effect.

They continued to mosey along the sun-baked main street, lined with a motley selection of wooden-constructed buildings. Redwood was the predominant feature, which gave a sturdy wholesomeness to the town's character. It appeared to have one of every kind of business people would need, including a blacksmith shop and livery stable, a saloon, hotel, bakery, and mercantile and general supply store. And at the far end of the main street stood a white-painted meeting house with a rooftop bell which doubled as a school and the local church.

'When ya found me, was there any sign of a horse? Perhaps it had wandered off a ways?'

'Nope, I didn't see no horse, mister. And you wasn't wearing a gun or holster either, which I thought was mighty strange 'cause you looked like a rough-hewn type to me.'

Barely were the words out the boy's mouth than he realized his honesty might have caused offence.

'But ya clean up real good, mister,' Derry added hastily, his hazel eyes anxiously wide.

'Don't worry, boy,' he smiled. 'I ain't offended.' Momentarily evaluating his appearance, he deduced there wasn't a hint of softness in him. 'Reckon I am the rough-hewn type.'

'There's nothin' wrong with that, mister — ' The boy broke off suddenly and gave him a thoughtful look. 'We'll have to give ya a name. I can't be callin' ya *mister* all the time. Besides, no one should be without a name, even if they have forgotten it.'

A name? Probably the boy was right. For the time being, he would need one.

'What name d'ya figure would suit me?'

Derry's eyes studied the man's features for a long moment. 'Somethin' special. And somethin' beginnin' with the letter J.'

'The letter J?'

'Well you got one of them tattoos on your shoulder,' Derry pointed up at the man's right shoulder. 'I seen it when you was lying in bed with your shirt off.'

He immediately pulled his coat and shirt away from his shoulder to reveal a small initial J tattoo. He felt it should have prompted some shred of recollection, but it didn't. The disappointment showed in his face and suddenly the town was too public a place for such private discoveries.

'Don't worry,' the boy spoke kindly, 'Pa says your memory will get better, and he's the best doctor for miles around. I'm goin' to be just like him when I'm all grown up,' Derry announced proudly. 'And Amber, she's already a fine medical assistant.'

He absorbed what the boy said, but a need for more privacy took precedence. 'Maybe we should be goin' back to the house?'

The boy agreed, and they turned in their tracks and headed back. 'Amber's also a great cook,' Derry grinned as he strode alongside. 'An' she's making something mighty tasty for supper tonight, Jay.'

And the name stuck. Jay it was. Just Jay.

★ ★ ★

Supper lived up to expectations. Amber had made a tasty beef stew with mashed potatoes and corn bread, followed by apple pie and plenty of good coffee. It was served in the main room of the Laineys' comfortably

11

furnished house, with the room being lit by the warm yellow glow of two coal-oil lamps. A polished mahogany dining-table assumed pride of place, spaciously seating Doc Evett Lainey, Amber, Derry and Jay.

Despite the delicious meal, friendly company and polite conversation, the event of sitting down to a family supper seemed to be an unfamiliar experience to Jay, and he wasn't entirely comfortable with the situation. Nevertheless, he'd done his best to look presentable. He'd shaved the stubble from his harsh yet handsomely sculptured face and slicked back his rich, sable hair, in an attempt to look less rough-hewn, but his sun-darkened skin and tall, broad-shouldered, leanly muscular physique needed more taming than he was capable of.

'Apart from getting your memory back,' Doc Lainey commented as they finished the remains of the meal, 'there's also the practical matters that have to be dealt with.' He went on to elaborate on what these were. 'You'll need money to live on, somewhere to stay, a horse, and other things a man needs to survive in these parts. Certainly, you're welcome to bunk here until you get back on your feet and I can lend you some money — '

Jay interrupted, 'I cain't be acceptin' any money from you folks. You've already been a great help to me and I don't intend imposin' on your hospitality any longer.'

'Oh, you're not imposing,' Amber insisted. 'We're doin' what any dutiful folks would do when someone's down on their luck through no fault of their own.'

She was wearing a beautiful blue dress tonight and her hair shone in soft liquid gold waves from the blue ribbon which tied it back from her heart-shaped face. Jay sighed inwardly. She was almost too good to look at. Frequently throughout the meal, he'd deliberately kept his eyes from lingering too long on her loveliness for fear his

13

desires might show and cause offence.

'You're decent folk, and I thank you for your hospitality, but I intend looking fer work to pay my own way in this town before movin' on,' Jay explained his intentions.

Doc Lainey nodded. 'A man's pride is all fine and well, and I understand what you're saying, but I insist you live under my roof at least until you find work. And maybe I can help you there too; some neigbours of ours have been on the lookout for extra hands to work on their ranch, and I'm sure they'd be glad of a strong feller like you. I could introduce you tomorrow and explain your circumstances.'

'I'd be much obliged,' Jay was pleased to accept the offer.

'Pa will tell 'em you ain't no outlaw,' Derry chipped in, trying to be helpful.

'That will do,' Amber chided her brother. 'Jay is obviously not an outlaw.'

'I didn't mean no insult to Jay, 'cause I like him, but none of us

14

knows for sure he ain't a wanted gunman; even Jay doesn't know who he is,' Derry reasoned.

'Well I'm a very good judge of character,' Amber argued. 'And if Jay had a shady past, I'd know it. Women can always sense these things.'

Her defence of Jay was a little more forceful than it should have been, unless she was secretly attracted to him, which of course, she was. A blush rose in her cheeks as she realized she'd made her feelings for him rather obvious to all concerned. Her father, brother and Jay pretended not to notice which, in itself, was silent and embarrassing testimony to the fact.

'Maybe you've got a wife and family of your own?' Derry blurted out a suggestion that served to fan the flames of Amber's embarrassment, which she was doing her darnedest to hide behind a calm façade and despite rose-bright cheeks.

Jay was inclined to disagree. 'Somehow, I don't think so. I don't feel married.'

His timber-deep voice spoke the word *married* as if it was anathema.

'You never can tell,' the doc backed up Derry's suggestion. 'I'd estimate you to be in your late twenties to early thirties, and you're a fine-looking feller, so the chances are you could be married.'

The doc turned to his daughter and said teasingly, 'What does your woman's intuition sense about Jay having a wife?'

Amber sunk her father with a withering look before addressing all three males at the dinner-table. 'I'm just thankful I'm not wed, 'cause most men aren't worth the trouble they bring to us women.' With that scathing comment, she went to make a fresh pot of coffee in the kitchen.

Jay hoped her ire wasn't entirely directed towards him, though he wasn't certain why she was riled.

'Don't worry,' Derry whispered to Jay, 'when a woman gets angry like that, it means she likes ya.'

Jay smiled at the boy's attempted wisdom regarding the female gender. Memory or no memory, Jay reckoned women were as unpredictable as a summer thunderstorm and he was certain he'd never ever fathom them out. Derry probably understood his sister's moods very well, and it was warming to imagine that she kinda liked him, though where such feelings could lead, he couldn't presume to surmise. When he got his memory back, there was no telling what his past might divulge. Until he knew who and what he was, he didn't dare harbour any romantic notions for Amber Lainey.

* * *

So, here he was, standing alone in the deep velvet stillness of the night, gazing into the far distance. The gold and rose sunset had now darkened to a purple and midnight-blue aurora. Even the languid breeze had gone to sleep.

Slumber had escaped Jay. Far too

restless to sleep, he'd slipped silently out of the house where the Laineys had kindly let him bed down for the night. From his vantage point, he could see the lights of Copperstone's town flickering way below the hillside.

Suddenly, amid the stillness, something stirred behind him in the long grass.

Whirring round to face the threat, instinct made him reach for his gun, which wasn't there. Luckily, there was no real danger; the noise he'd heard was simply a night-time varmint which was more scared of Jay than he was of it, and scurried back into the darkness from which it came.

In that instant, he realized something about himself: even though he wasn't wearing a gun, it was mightly clear he was used to having one around — and the lightning speed with which he'd reached for it indicated he was a fast draw. Very fast.

What kind of man did that make him? he wondered, tension gripping hold of his guts and twisting them tight. An outlaw, or an upholder of the law, or maybe just a feller who was adept at protecting himself? He didn't have any answers, but the reality remained — he was incredibly fast with a gun, and there had to be a good reason for this ability. Even if it was a bad reason.

2

By sun-up, Jay was back at the Lainey house, sitting on the front porch, as if he'd simply risen at the crack of dawn and was waiting for the rest of the occupants to awaken. The house was right in the hub of Copperstone and Jay sat on the porch steps watching the town slowly come to life.

A raw, dazzling brilliance was a sure sign that the day was going to be a real scorcher. The sun, a gleaming white-hot gold, bolstered Jay's hopes of the new day shedding some light on his past.

Although he hadn't had a wink of sleep, adrenalin was keeping him alert. He felt as if he were waiting on something, something vital, which of course he was. Apprehensively, he was waiting on his past to catch up with him. But there was something else, in the dark recesses of his memory ... a feeling deep in the pit of his guts, coiled like a rattle-snake waiting to strike.

Squinting against the sunlight, he noticed a man eyeing him from the other side of the street, and making no secret of it. Standing outside the mercantile, the stranger was givin' him a bone-breakin' stare. He was swarthy, wearing a sombrero, high-holstered pistols, and a mean expression.

For several pulsing seconds, their vision clashed. The emotion in the man's jet-black eyes was as cold as the day was hot.

Jay stood up, undecided whether or not to cross the street and approach him. The man obviously recognized him and, for whatever reason, hated him on sight.

Anticipating Jay's approach, the man immediately mounted his pinto and rode off, heading out of town, kicking up a cloud of angry dust in his wake.

'Who was that?' Derry's young voice

gasped, drawing Jay's attention away from the departing Mexican. Derry had been standing in the open doorway behind Jay. 'He was staring at ya real hard.'

'I dunno,' Jay replied, wishing he did know, instinct warning him it wouldn't be too long before he found out.

'If looks could kill, ya'd be a dead man,' the boy exclaimed, seeming to shudder at the prospect.

'Well they cain't and I ain't.' Jay's response was casual, but only on the surface. Underneath the calm exterior, every nerve in his body was on red alert.

'Reckon he'll come back to git ya?'

Jay soothed the boy's trepidation. 'Nah, I shouldn't think I'll be seein' him again,' said Jay, nothing in his strong face betraying his doubt.

'Amber says breakfast's ready.' Derry brightened, eagerly prepared to take Jay's word that nothing was wrong.

Derry led the way inside to the kitchen where Amber and Doc Lainey were already seated and tucking in.

'Help yourself to coffee,' Amber instructed Jay, pointing to a pot on the kitchen stove.

He did, then seated himself down to breakfast. A hearty plate of bacon, eggs and fried bread was already laid out for him.

'How's your head this mornin'?' asked the doc.

Jay gave it a reassuring rub. 'Feels almost better.'

Doc Lainey leaned across to double-check. 'The swelling seems to have subsided,' he confirmed, prodding the bump. 'Another day or two and you'll be as right as rain. Except of course, for your memory, but that'll come back in time.'

A shadow passed over Jay's face, as if something dark had crossed his soul. He chose his words carefully before asking, 'Even if a man had lost his memory, would he know whether his past was good or bad?'

'You're asking me whether or not

you could be a bad 'un?' the doc summarized.

Jay nodded briefly.

'Depends on what you consider bad,' Doc Lainey hedged. 'Ya see, it's possible, though I'm not sayin' you did, that you killed somebody and don't remember. Now that's only bad if ya killed 'em other than in self-defence and there was no other choice. If it was self-defence, that don't make you a bad person.' He hesitated, hoping he'd made his point understood, before concluding, 'From everything I know about amnesia, a man can usually tell whether he has a black heart or a pure one. And, as far as I can figure, you ain't black-hearted.'

The doc's opinion was just the balm Jay needed to help push any worrisome notions to the back of his mind, at least for the present.

'Father's going to take you over to the Mistral Ranch this morning to meet the Garrett family,' Amber enlightened Jay on the day's itinerary. 'Likely they'll give you a job.' Her tone was light and breezy, as if the idea of him staying awhile in Copperstone Creek appealed to her.

Jay's green eyes surveyed her under thick black lashes. She was wearing a pink dress this morning, and he pondered whether she had one for every colour of the rainbow? If he had it in his power, he'd buy her all the pretty dresses she wanted and all the ribbons to match.

Topaz eyes viewed him unblinkingly across the table as she awaited his reponse to her statement, trying to ignore the prolonged and intense scrutiny his eyes were directing at her.

Reacting to her expression, Jay jerked his mouth into action. 'I'd be much obliged.' Time just seemed to stand stock-still whenever he looked at her and his mind wandered way off the main track. Without a doubt, Amber was the type of woman who could derail him without even trying. How easy it would be to fall deeply in love with her. And, unless he was mistaken, Amber's heart was struggling against succumbing to his dark and mysterious sensuality.

It was then he decided it wouldn't be right to encourage a young woman's affections, to entice her heart into danger. Much as it hurt him to shatter her illusions, this was neither the place nor the time to go a-courting.

'Reckon I won't be hangin' around Copperstone for too long,' Jay dashed her hopes. 'Once my memory's restored, I'll be movin' on.'

He deliberately dropped her heart from a great height, and although neither a word or gesture from her flinched, he sensed her drowning in her own internal tears.

The Mistral ranch was on the outskirts of town, a fair-sized property set amid a flat expanse of plain. Copperstone's river touched one edge of the ranch where the grass was greener under a canopy of juniper trees.

Doc Lainey took Jay over in his

horse and buggy, having kindly given him a well-worn leather bag containing a collarless pale-blue shirt, shaving kit and a few necessary odds and ends to help him out.

After explaining the circumstances to the Mistral's owner, Chuck Garrett and his wife, Verity, the doc returned home, leaving Jay at the ranch. The Garretts had been mighty pleased to take him on, though their charge-hand, Tug Deakin, had been less enthusiastic. Abruptly, he'd excused himself from the proceedings after hearing all he needed, or wanted, from Doc Lainey. At best, Deakin was a man of few words, and this morning, his silent opinion had spoken volumes.

'Good help is scarce,' Chuck Garrett admitted to Jay, as they sat on the ranchhouse porch discussing their business. 'We sure could use ya.' Garrett stood up and held out a hand that was as large and steady as Jay's.

Rising to his feet, Jay gripped

Garrett's hand firmly. 'I'm grateful for the work.'

Having secured their agreement on a handshake, they then walked outside across the yard towards the bunkhouse. Chuck Garrett was a robust, square-set man in his early fifties. Greying brown hair poked out from under his stetson and his moustache was a feature in itself, resembling a pair of buffalo horns turned upside down. His ruddy face was seamed with deep-etched lines like a sun-dried riverbed, and life's trials and tribulations had watered-down his eyes to an almost colourless blue, but Jay got the impression they still didn't miss a trick.

'The hours are long, but the pay's fair, and we'll feed ya and give ya a place to bunk.' Garrett pointed towards a log-built bunkhouse adjacent to the painted timber ranchhouse. The bunkhouse consisted of two large log cabins adjoined by a dog-trot. A shelf ran along the outside of one half of the cabins where a number of bare-chested ranch-hands were shaving, using the shelf to rest their soap, brushes, shaving mugs and razors.

Several sets of unwelcoming eyes turned to glare at Jay. It was hate at first sight, at least on their part. Either too fat, or too darn skinny, Jay inwardly applauded their nerve at standing there trying to look tough.

Deakin stood beside them, the smug expression on his chiselled face indicating his triumph at having poisoned the men against Jay before they'd had a chance to get properly acquainted.

Jay sensed they intended giving him a hard time, but for some inexplicable reason, maybe a quirk in his nature, he didn't give a damn.

Garrett halted and spoke in a low tone just out of earshot of the other men. 'Bein' as you're a friend of Doc Lainey, and 'cause of your predicament, I'm prepared to advance ya a month's wages.'

'That's mighty decent of ya, I won't let ya down.'

'Don't go tellin' the boys,' Garrett confided. 'They can be a wordy lot when they're riled, but I need 'em to work the ranch. And take no mind of Tug Deakin, he don't like nobody. Indifference is as good as ya'll git.' Garrett passed Jay a sly wink.

'Ah git your drift,' Jay nodded.

'This here's Jay,' Garrett announced to the men. 'He's gonna be workin' here awhile.'

There was a low rumble of acknowledgement, not to Jay, but to Garrett.

Garrett then addressed Deakin. 'As charge-hand, see he gits his share of the tasks,' he ordered, before walking back to the ranchhouse.

'Sure, boss,' Deakin confirmed with vicious glee behind Garrett's retreating figure.

Jay had a bad feeling. Garrett had just given Deakin a big stick with which to beat him. He cussed inwardly. Life at the Mistral Ranch was gonna be a heck of a time. The charge-hand would make sure of that.

Tug Deakin matched Jay in years, and stature, but bitterness had gnawed his hawkish features into an ageing grimace. The bitterness seemed to run in rivulets down his face, the furrowed lines ending at the precipice of a pointed chin. Inborn resentment towards most things had dragged his features downwards, and his character with it. Even his overly broad shoulders sloped at a pessimistic angle, but Deakin bore the inclined posture with a fierce defiance.

The dark figure of Deakin approached Jay, his cold grey eyes lancing him to the core. 'Ya better tread warily,' Deakin rasped in warning. 'We don't cotton to strangers round here, especially when they're as strange as you.'

The gibe richocheted off Jay's untrammelled masculinity, hitting Deakin straight in the eye.

The strength of Jay's wordless parry gave the charge-hand pause for thought.

31

'He looks real shifty ta me, Deakin,' a skinny cowboy threw his opinion of Jay into the ring, safety in numbers being the reason for his bravado.

'Garrett must have a soft spot for stray vermin,' another chimed in, ridiculing Jay, 'because I smell a rat.'

A sneer rippled through the men as each one condemned him without justice. Clearly, they were spoiling for a fight, mistaking him for an easy target on whom to vent their resentment.

Up to a point, Jay understood their animosity, though he didn't like it one iota. And if he hadn't been desperate for work, he'd have spat the threats back in their faces and left the ranch there and then.

'For all we know, we could be sharing a bunkhouse with a rustler, an outlaw or a cold-blooded murderer,' Deakin sniped.

'Better hope I'm not a murderer,' Jay retorted, low and deep. 'Nor give me any reason to become one,' he added,

Bodine, well, he'll likely try to git on your good side. He won't want to cross the likes of you again.'

'With any luck, I'll be gone quite soon. Once I git my memory back, I'm heading outa here to wherever I really belong.'

Corey viewed him sceptically. 'Some men don't belong anywhere. They jest drift from town to town.'

'I don't feel like no drifter,' Jay commented as they reached the ranchhouse where Verity Garrett was standing alert on the front porch.

'Where's Pa?' Corey called out to his mother.

'He's headed over to the south range,' she replied, eyeing Jay as she spoke. 'What happened?'

'Deakin and the boys got outa hand. Bodine cut Jay's arm with a knife,' he explained briefly. 'Could ya fix him up while I git the horses ready? Jay's working with me today.'

Verity, a small, slight but tenacious looking woman, wanted more details.

43

'Jay will tell you all about it while you're fixin' his arm,' Corey promised, leaving Jay to do just that.

Verity cleaned the wound which wasn't as bad as the amount of blood on the remains of his shirt sleeve suggested. She was kind, and keen to hear Jay's version of the story as she wrapped a bandage around his arm.

'Is this the reason they call you J?' she asked, seeing the tattoo.

'Yes ma'am. It was Doc Lainey's boy who came up with the idea of callin' me Jay. But I'm hoping it won't be long before I know what the initial J really stands for.'

Verity finished bandaging his wound and looked him straight in the eye. 'Jay suits ya,' she confirmed. 'Although I knew a man once who had his sweetheart's name tattooed on his forearm.'

She looked away now, unable to hold his gaze, and he suspected she might be talking about herself.

'Verity is a mighty pretty name for

any man to wear on his arm,' Jay grinned.

'Don't you go mentioning this to Chuck,' she whispered, trying to contain her own secret smile. 'We've been married for more than thirty years but he still gets jealous about my first beau.'

Jay's green eyes lit up with his smile. 'I won't ever say a word.'

'Say a word about what?' Corey walked in on their conversation.

'About nothin',' his mother nipped Corey's question in the bud. 'Jay's all fixed up, so you two can be getting on with the ranching and let me get on with my own chores.'

'Thanks Ma,' Corey acknowledged, then turned to Jay who was wearing the clean shirt Doc Lainey had given him. 'Come on, I got a mustang saddled and ready for ya.'

Outside, Corey mounted his roan and Jay did likewise on to the mustang.

'Some of the fences on the north side need mendin'. You can give me a hand,' Corey told him as they rode north together.

'I cain't imagine what it must be like not to know who ya are.' Corey seemed unable to fathom Jay's situation.

'I'd never have believed it possible,' Jay admitted. 'It's hard to explain what it's like.'

'Well, you sure know how to fist fight, and ride as good as any ranch-hand round these parts,' Corey credited him. 'If you're good at mending fences, Deakin better watch out you don't git his job.'

Jay sensed the comment was made half in jest and half in earnest, but he really had no intention of staying in Copperstone that long.

'As I said before, I'll be movin' on soon, but I appreciate your being fair-minded about everything, Corey.'

'Ya never can tell how things will work out,' Corey concluded. 'Pa don't like Deakin any more than I do. If the truth be known, we'd be glad to see the back of him — if we'd a suitable replacement. Maybe ranching's in your blood?'

'Ya never can tell,' Jay echoed, trying to keep an open mind, but doubting this was where his future lay.

★ ★ ★

Corey had to show Jay how to mend any gaps in the fences, but he proved to be a quick learner and a tireless worker.

Later, back at the bunkhouse, Deakin and Bondine were resting from their injuries. No words were exchanged between Deakin and Jay, just a grudging silence which spoke volumes. The other ranch-hands made no bones about the situation, though they did tread warily around Jay. Bodine, true to Corey's prediction, tried to make friends with Jay. He didn't want a friend like Bodine, but with allies thin on the ground, he didn't need another enemy. They shook hands over their differences, a gesture which Bodine wrongly assumed made them friends.

Jay chose a bunk for himself at the far corner of the cabin away from the others. Here he ate a plateful of stew and bread, washed down with coffee. He kept to himself, and that's the way he planned to continue while he was here.

After supper, Jay assisted Corey and Chuck Garrett secure the horses in the corral for the evening.

'I've told the boys I want no more trouble, so you shouldn't have any problems sharing the bunkhouse,' Chuck avowed to Jay before he and Corey retired to the ranchhouse.

'We've got an early start tomorrow, Jay,' Corey added. 'Git some shut-eye.'

'See ya in the mornin',' Jay affirmed, walking away into the darkness, guided only by a dim light glowing from the bunkhouse.

His thoughts were rewinding the day's events, when a faint noise triggered a disturbing warning. Halting in his tracks, he listened warily. There was nothing but silence — and darkness.

In that instant, something flickered in his mind, as if the chord of a distant memory had been stirred. What it was, he couldn't fathom, but something in his bones told him it was vital to his survival.

Walking on, the whispered sounds followed his every step, almost as if something invisible were pursuing him.

Keeping a strong, steady pace, he continued towards the bunkhouse, heaving an inner sigh of relief when he reached it safely. Deakin, Bodine and the others were all present and accounted for. Whoever, or whatever, was outside lurking in the shadows, was a stranger. It certainly wasn't the Garretts, for he'd seen them go into the ranchhouse.

Reining his stray thoughts together, he considered that he might be just plain dog-tired. Unsure, he decided to give himself the benefit of the doubt.

So, attributing it to lack of sleep, he settled down for the night.

Lying in bed, his thoughts returned again to recent events, which were his only real memories.

At the end of his first day at the Mistral ranch, he concluded that little light had been shed on his past — but he had the feeling he was at least one day closer to remembering something important. Something which might save his life.

3

Jay's sleep was disturbed by nightmares. Several times during the night, he awoke in a cold sweat, only to go back to sleep again to dream the same nightmare over and over again.

The ranch-hands were none the wiser, grunting and snoring like pigs within dreams of their own.

Once though, in the darkness, lit only by the shards of moonlight streaming through the windows, Jay caught Deakin's pale-grey eyes silently watching him from the other end of the cabin.

★ ★ ★

Jay was up before any of the other men, rising early with the first light of dawn. Outside, he washed and shaved in the warm morning air. Pouring buckets of water over himself, he dowsed away the salty scent of sweat, letting the sun dry his body and dripping-wet head of rich dark hair. In a way, he also hoped it would dilute the ghoulish dreams which still lingered on him, and wash away the uneasy feeling which was hard to shake off.

The nightmare certainly seemed less gruesome in the daylight, but it bothered him none the less. It had been a strange, sinister dream, centred around a silver skeleton, whose metal bones jangled every nerve in his body as they moved. Each time the nightmare ended when the skeleton drew a silvergrip pistol from nowhere and shot Jay dead in the chest. Repeatedly, the shock of the bullet, even though only a dream, woke him up.

'Your memory starting to come back to haunt you?' Deakin's bitter-tipped voice came up from behind him, his nose a mash of purple bruises and dried blood.

The snide remark did not justify

a reply, and Jay continued shaving. Wearing only his jeans, his leanly muscled torso showed no marked sign of brusing, glistening wet where he'd dowsed it. The cut on his arm had sealed itself into a thin red line which required no further bandaging. This was something else he'd learned about himself — he was a fast healer. So, maybe it wouldn't be too long before his memory healed too? It was an optimistic thought, but he didn't have a chance to dwell on it because Deakin was spoiling for more trouble.

'They say a man cain't sleep when his conscience is pressing down on his brain an' tightenin' like a vice,' Deakin salivated. 'Wonder what deep, dark secret's keepin' you awake at night?'

'Maybe the same thing that's bothering you,' Jay cast back at him. 'Unless you sleep with your eyes open.'

'My conscience is clear,' Deakin retorted. 'And unlike you, I've got a *long memory* — an' I ain't forgettin' what you did yesterday.'

Jay plunged his soapy razor into a bucket of water, lifting it out dripping wet and glinting steel sharp in the sunlight. 'Neither am I an' I got a lot more room for keeping memories fresh than you have,' Jay menaced, watching the Adam's apple in Deakin's throat constrict involuntarily.

The air burned with Deakin's inner anger, tinged with hidden fear.

'You threatening me?' Deakin growled.

Jay's voice poured out vitriol, as thick and smooth as molasses. 'Do I need to?'

Grudgingly, Deakin backed away, realizing he'd antagonized Jay far enough for the time being. Dunking his head in a bucket of water, he surfaced and shook off the excess like a shaggy dog. His hatchet face glared daggers at Jay promising revenge at another place and time, before going quietly back inside the bunkhouse.

By the time the rest of the ranch-hands were getting up and washed, smoke was already billowing from the adjoining cabin — the cookhouse, a sure indication that breakfast was being rustled up by Lucky, the ranch-hands' cook.

Jay's belly was rumbling like rocks in an empty tin can, so he moseyed over to see what was cooking.

It was at that moment a horse and despatch rider approached the bunkhouse at speed.

'Where's Lucky?' the rider called out to Jay.

'Sorry, I'm new around here,' Jay apologized, seconds before an old man came scurrying out the cookhouse door, arms eager to collect whatever package the despatch rider had for him.

The exchange was so quick, Jay hardly had a chance to see what the rider, who was keen to be on his way to his next delivery, gave the old man, who, Jay reckoned must be Lucky. Grizzled grey with age, he had arms that were a shade too long for his short stature, and a voice as rough as sandpaper.

Jay followed him into the cookhouse, where the smell of bacon and coffee was making his mouth water.

Lucky was more concerned with tearing open the package.

Jay watched his heavily lined face smile excitedly, losing at least a decade in years as he examined what appeared to be a Bannerman's mail-order catalogue.

'I been waitin' months for this new catalogue,' Lucky admitted gleefully to Jay, as he hurriedly flicked through the pages searching for something in particular.

Jay's curiosity had been aroused. 'What ya lookin' fer?'

'The ladies' corset pages,' Lucky grinned, then added, 'You must be the new feller — the fist fighter.'

'I'm Jay,' he introduced himself, uneasy with the fist fighter reputation. 'I take it you're Lucky.'

'Certainly am today,' the old man chuckled. 'Take a gander at these beauties.' He held the catalogue open at a double page showing pictures of ladies wearing a selection of corsetry. 'Ain't they a sight for sore eyes?' he leered, straightening his spectacles, which were as thick as the bottom of two liquor bottles, for a better look.

Before Jay could reply, Lucky prattled on excitedly, 'My eyesight ain't as sharp as it used to be, but it does me fine for cookin' up the ranch grub — and admiring the women.'

Jay couldn't help smiling. It was the first time he'd felt like laughing in the past two days.

'Here,' Lucky thrust the catalogue at him. 'Rip the pages out an' pin 'em up on the wall fer me while I finish fixin' breakfast.'

Trying to hide his amusement, Jay carefully began tearing the pages, six in all, from the catalogue.

'Pin 'em over there.' Lucky pointed to the wall opposite the stove. 'Not too high up, I ain't as tall as you.'

A dried-out and faded catalogue corsetry picture was already hanging on the log cabin wall, curled up at the edges and crisp from the intense heat of the cookhouse. The wall also bore the tacks where other pictures had been but were now missing. Jay pinned the new ones up, ensuring they were within easy eyeball height for Lucky.

'Ah used to have plenty, but the fellers kept stealing 'em,' Lucky informed him. 'But I warned 'em if I catch 'em stealing any more I'll shoot their heads clean off their shoulders.' He indicated towards a sawn-off shotgun perched against a cupboard. 'Don't need good eyesight to shoot my old scatter-gun. It'll kill anything within blurring distance.

Jay laughed.

'The boys will be comin' fer their chow any minute, so if yer wantin' yer fair share, git a plate and pile it up now,' Lucky advised him, cooking up another large pan of bacon.

Jay helped himself to bacon, eggs and fried bread, then seated himself down at the big wooden table. The cookhouse was basic, with cupboards and shelves stacked with everything from sacks of flour to tinned beef. Pots and pans hung from a low beam, and a chimney pipe stuck out the top of the stove, rising right through the roof.

'This is mighty tasty,' Jay complimented Lucky on his cooking.

'I used to herd cattle halfways across the territory, 'till I got too old, worn and plum tuckered out,' Lucky summarized his existence. 'Cookin' suits me jest fine these days. Least I never go hungry.' He patted his belly. 'An' the pay's enough for a single man like me.'

'Ya ain't married?'

'I like women too much to marry jest one of them,' he jested.

'No woman would have an old dog like you,' Bodine joked, as he and the others swarmed in for breakfast like a flock of vultures.

'Bet ya I've had more pretty young women than you, Bodine,' Lucky gibed, waving a metal spatula at him to emphasize his remark.

'Yeh,' chimed in Deakin, 'Bodine only gits the ugly ones.'

Buoyant laughter lifted the atmosphere, and for a moment, Jay could see a better side to the ranch-hands.

Bodine chewed on a mouthful of bacon as he spluttered cheerfully, 'I'll tell ya somethin', it was worth gittin' punched by Jay here just to have Doc Lainey's daughter have her hands all over me.'

'Amber didn't look twice at you, Bodine. She was too taken with me,' Deakin declared. 'Maybe I should steal her affections away from Corey?'

Although Deakin's comment was made in fun, Jay realized that the man seemed to take it for granted that Amber was Corey Garrett's girl. Even though he had no claim to her affections, Jay felt a pang of jealousy stab him in the gut.

'Amber Lainey's too much of a lady for my taste,' said Lucky. 'Give me a real woman, like Lou-Lou at the Sundown saloon, any day.'

'Wonder what Amber would say if she knew her beau was seeing Lou-Lou behind her pretty little back?' Deakin mused spitefully.

'Who's Lou-Lou?' Jay asked Deakin, momentarily forgetting their differences.

'The best darn female in these here parts,' Deakin seemed proud to announce. 'But she wouldn't give a troublemaker like you a second glance.'

'I told ya yesterday, I ain't lookin' fer trouble,' Jay emphasized.

'You sure got a strange way of showin' it,' Deakin countered.

'You're the one who started it,' Jay defended, confounded that the blame was being put on him.

'I just don't like strangers,' Deakin spat.

'You just don't like nobody,' Jay cast at him accusingly. 'You don't even know me — none of ya do.'

Deakin actually smiled. 'Hell! You don't even know you.'

For some reason, stating their

differences cleared the air, and eased
the tension between Jay and Deakin.
The atmosphere was better, though the
rift wasn't completely healed.

★ ★ ★

After breakfast, Jay and Corey worked
the far side of the Mistral ranch range,
near the river. It was here, as they
stopped to water their horses in the
noonday sun, that Corey gave Jay the
advanced month's wages as promised.
'Pa said to give you this.' He pressed
the handful of dollars into Jay's palm.
'Later, you can head into town and
pick up anything you need.'

'I'm mighty grateful,' Jay acknowledged,
putting the money safely in the pocket
of his jeans.

'A gun holster will set you back a
month's wages, but I've got one you
can borrow 'till then. Don't seem right
a man not having a gun.' Corey then
took a pistol and holster out of his
saddle-bag and handed them over. 'It's

a .44 Smith and Wesson. Should do ya just fine.'

It was the words Smith and Wesson which triggered Jay's memory. And when he held the pistol in his hand, something clicked into place.

'Somethin' the matter?' Corey asked, seeing the faraway look in Jay's eyes.

Jay pulled his distant thoughts back to the present. 'This Smith and Wesson reminds me of something . . . ' His voice trailed off as he tried to remember what it was.

'Maybe ya used to have one,' Corey suggested, taking a large gulp of water from his flask.

Jay closed his hand around the gun's ivory grip, getting a real good feel of its weight and balance. 'Maybe,' he agreed, almost convinced that this was true.

'There's one sure way to find out,' Corey enthused, drawing his Colt .45. 'See that juniper tree over there?' He pointed towards a particular tree on the opposite side of the river that had a sign nailed to it, bearing the Mistral ranch name. 'If you can hit that sign with the Smith and Wesson and outshoot me and my Colt, then we'll know for certain. But I warn ya, I'm a darn good shot.'

Jay strapped on the gun. It sat snug in the leather holster at his right hip.

'Ya ready, Jay?'

'Yep.'

Corey was the first to shoot. His discharged bullet hit the sign, just right off centre. He seemed pleased with the result. 'Now it's your turn.'

Jay's head was thumping and blood thudded through his body, as if everything inside him was being turned backwards to another place and time. With one controlled breath, he drew the pistol clean out of the holster in a swift movement, fired direct into the centre of the sign, then replaced the gun just as quickly back in its holster.

Corey was impressed. 'Best of three?' he said, extending the challenge.

Jay agreed.

Corey fired two more shots, both again striking just right of their target mark. 'Think ya can beat that?' he grinned.

Jay knew he could.

Without hesitation, he drew his pistol and fired twice. Both bullets landed dead centre, causing the wooden sign to almost split in half.

'Never seen shootin' like that since we'd a fast-gun outlaw in Copperstone a few years back,' Corey gasped. 'He was fast, but I'd put my money on you bein' quicker.'

'Maybe I shouldn't be havin' this gun.' Jay offered to give it back, reluctant to bear a weapon which he could wield so effectively, especially as he still didn't know who, or what, he was. He'd suspected he was fast with a gun that first evening he'd made to draw when he heard a noise in the darkness. But he never imagined he'd be quite so fast — or accurate. This kind of shooting put him in a different category from most men, and all the niggling doubts about his character came flooding back, threatening to drown any hope he had of being a law-abiding man.

Corey refused to take the gun off him. 'Nah, you keep it, Jay. If you can shoot like that, there must be a good reason for it.'

'Or a bad reason,' Jay suggested wryly.

'I trust ya, Jay. But I don't think we should make it public knowledge that you're a fast draw. That would really be asking for trouble,' Corey advised sensibly.

'Trouble's the last thing I need. Got me enough as it is.'

For the next two hours, they continued working, riding the range rounding up some stray horses. With Jay's help, Corey was able to finish the tasks early, which allowed Jay to head into town by late afternoon.

Trouble was waiting for him — and so was another clue to his past.

4

Copperstone was winding down for the day, as if the town was taking a breather, ready to come alive again at night. The unhurried pace of the townsfolk was infectious, causing Jay to fall in step with their slow, easy rhythm.

Jay sauntered across the main street, heading for the mercantile, where he intended buying himself a new shirt and one or two other pieces of clothing from his wages.

Coming out of the mercantile were Amber and Derry Lainey. Amber stiffened on seeing Jay, but pretended she hadn't noticed him.

'Look Amber, there's Jay,' Derry pointed, making it impossible for her to ignore him.

Jay approached the door of the mercantile, well aware of Amber's adverse reaction.

'Hiya, Jay,' Derry beamed. 'Heard about you beatin' those guys with your bare fists,' the boy enthused, punching the air in imitation of the fight.

'Behave yourself,' Amber scolded her younger brother, clearly unamused by such antics. 'I'm sorry, we're in a hurry,' she apologized, as she grabbed Derry by the hand and side-stepped Jay. 'I'm delivering some medicine to one of father's patients.' With that, she hurried off, trying to prevent Derry from turning back to stare.

It was clear to Jay that it was an excuse, rather than an apology. The wary expression in her topaz eyes said it all. He knew what she was thinking. She'd tended the wounds of Deakin and Bodine, and any trust she'd had in him had waned. He would never forget that look on her lovely face. She was questioning whether he really was an outlaw — which caused him to question himself. If decent folks like the Laineys were deliberately avoiding him, maybe they had good reason?

Feeling somewhat degraded and dispirited, Jay entered the mercantile, which was relatively quiet. Browsing through the clothing section, he had an uneasy feeling he was being watched.

Turning round, he saw the swarthy Mexican he'd seen the day before, glaring at him from the other side of the store. His sombrero hung by a strap down his back, revealing he had a head of thick blue-black hair.

Slowly and deliberately, the Mexican approached Jay, as if to menace him.

Jay stood his ground. Fate intended him to meet this Mexican, and he wasn't about to run away from the confrontation.

The few remaining customers must have sensed there was trouble brewing, because they quickly made themselves scarce. The bespectacled storekeeper stayed a safe distance behind his solid wooden counter.

The dull, hollow thud of the Mexican's boots echoed in the quietness, but there was another sound, almost inaudible, which sent a shiver of realization along Jay's spine. It was the same noise he'd heard last night in the darkness at the Mistral ranch.

As the Mexican neared him, Jay saw where the strange sound was coming from. On the sleeve of the Mexican's embroidered bolero jacket hung a small silver skeleton lucky charm. The bones of the skeleton jingled whenever the Mexican moved.

That's when something significant clicked into place within Jay's mind. The silver skeleton he'd dreamt about must be linked to the Mexican, who also happened to wear high-holstered pistols with silver grips. In the nightmare, the skeleton had shot him in the chest with a silver-grip pistol. It was too strong a coincidence to be just a dream. It was probably his memory trying to warn him about who the Mexican really was, and obviously, it was he who had been prowling around the Mistral ranch last night. But why?

The Mexican halted near Jay and stared at him with cold, jet-black eyes. Only a table piled with shirts and jeans separated them.

'Remember me?' the Mexican rasped, the deep scar across his left cheekbone drawn tight.

Jay stepped out from behind the table, revealing he was wearing the Smith and Wesson.

This seemed to tame the Mexican's bravado slightly. His dark eyes displayed a flicker of surprise when he surveyed Jay's gun, and he took a cautious step backwards.

'Who are ya?' Jay demanded, low and unfearful.

The Mexican didn't answer.

'What were ya doin' prowlin' around the Mistral last night?'

Jay's forthright question took the Mexican aback, but he tried to pretend otherwise. 'I was looking for you.'

'Well, ya found me now. So, spit it out, what d'ya want?'

Black jets glared hard into the depths

of Jay's green eyes. 'I just wanted to look you straight in the face to make sure you are who I think you are.'

'And who might that be?'

'Silvano!' A defiant man's voice shouted from the front door of the mercantile.

The Mexican pivoted round immediately in answer to his name.

Standing in the sun-shadowed doorway was a tall, lean man, dressed in black. The wide brim of his black stetson hid his features.

'Let's go,' the shadowed stranger beckoned abruptly to Silvano.

'We will meet again,' Silvano promised menacingly to Jay, before leaving hastily.

Silvano? Jay turned the name over and over in his mind. It had a familiar ring, but he couldn't quite grasp who he was.

'Know who either of those men are?' Jay asked the store-keeper.

'Nope, and I don't know you either, mister,' he replied nervously.

'My name's Jay, and I'm workin' the Mistral Ranch,' he calmed the store-keeper's anxiety. 'And I need to buy myself some new clothes.'

'Then ya came to the right place,' the man brightened, keen to help him select

★ ★ ★

'Sure he didn't recognize ya?' Lorn Catlin asked Silvano as they rode together out of town.

'He don't remember nothin',' Silvano confirmed.

'Seems too easy,' Lorn commented. 'Maybe he's tryin' ta fool us?'

The Mexican shook his head.

Lorn's lean-boned face broke into a sly smile beneath his black stetson. 'Let's go tell the boys.'

Lorn and Silvano headed for a secluded cabin on the fringe of Copperstone where the rest of their outlaw gang were staying.

'Did ya see him?' Roscoe Nash was

eager to question Lorn. 'Did ya git a good look at him?'

'Yeh, but Silvano was the one who spoke to him,' Lorn replied.

'Did he see both of ya?' Sparks Becker chimed in.

Roscoe and Sparks were both members of Lorn Catlin's outlaw gang. So too were Silvano Garcia and Yerby the Kid. All of them were in their mid to late twenties, except for nineteen-year-old Yerby.

'I kept my distance,' Lorn explained. 'I never did trust that one.'

'He's lost his memory all right,' Silvano asserted. 'I looked him straight in the eye and asked him if he remembered me, and he just stared at me real blank.'

'He knew ya were at the Mistral last night,' Lorn reminded him and enlightened the others.

'Sure he ain't tryin' ta trick us?' Roscoe pushed for reassurance. Roscoe was the cautious one. A born worrier, thin as a lath, without an ounce of flesh to spare, and a brown, stringy moustache.

'It sounds too good to be true,' Sparks remarked.

'Believe it,' said Silvano.

Sparks was so-called because he liked to spark his spurs on anything solid. And solid described his build quite aptly. Stout-timbered, Sparks had a sawn-off face comprised of squashed features and a blunted nose.

In comparison, Lorn Catlin was almost handsome. Almost. Narrow green eyes were set in a rawboned face. Dark hair and a long-legged, rangy build were emphasized by the dark clothes he always wore. From his long flowing coat to his stetson, everything was black. Overall, Lorn Catlin made quite a striking figure.

Then there was Kid Yerby. Many men had let the Kid's fresh-faced, innocent blond appearance fool them. And most of those fools were now lying toes up in the bone-orchard. Lorn liked to brag that he himself was a born outlaw, but Kid Yerby was equally so. Roscoe and Sparks sort of drifted that way and unintentionally ended up on the wrong side of the law. And as for Silvano, well, he was simply a law unto himself.

Altogether they were a mismatched five-strong gang, who had more than a passing interest in Jay's lost memory.

'What d'ya plan on doin', Lorn?' the kid spoke up.

A sardonic smile crossed Lorn's face. 'I plan on gittin' even.'

* * *

Jay paid for his goods at the mercantile, then left. He intended going straight back to the ranch, but the town's saloon seemed to beckon him like a cool-running stream to a thirsty horse.

Leaving his purchases tied to his horse, he moseyed over to the Sundown saloon. Pushing open the batwing doors, he strode inside. A large mirror hung above the bar, and he couldn't help but look at his reflection and wonder exactly who he was. It was a peculiar sensation to see himself as a stranger. He felt an eerie sense of dislocation, cut adrift from the rest of the world.

He bought himself a beer and sat down at an empty table. Several fellers were playing cards, but apart from them, the saloon was quiet. No doubt it would be busy in the evening, after the townsfolk had finished their day's work.

The beer was cool and refreshing, quenching both his thirst and his uneasiness. A dozen questions buzzed inside his head, and he didn't have any answers. The Smith and Wesson, and Silvano, definitely rang a bell in the clouded recesses of his mind.

If only he could remember . . .

It was then he got his first glimpse of Lou-Lou — and instantly she knocked every other thought clean out of his head.

A luscious blond, Lou-Lou shimmered

down the stairs of the saloon in a dress that looked as if it were forged from starlight. More stunning than pretty, Lou-Lou's womanly allure made her seem far lovelier than she really was. So powerful was her magnetic attraction, a man daren't doubt her beauty.

Deakin and Lucky hadn't exaggerated their acclaim of her, Jay concurred. Lou-Lou was stunning, and her confidence showed she was accustomed to the effect her spectacular looks had on men.

He watched her survey every man in the saloon, then, to his dismay, she walked straight towards him, coming to a shimmering pause at his table. Up close, he saw her eyes were a smouldering blue fire, tempered by the coolness of her barely-blond hair. This was a woman who blew hot and cold, controlling a man's temperature by her womanly will.

'You the fist-fighter?' she asked, in a real sassy manner.

Jay almost choked on the mouthful

of beer he hadn't yet swallowed.

'Don't choke on it honey, jest drink it,' her full, rosy-lipped mouth quipped dryly.

'I seem to have wrongly acquired a bad reputation.' Jay tried to shake off his fist-fighter renown.

'I like a man who's modest,' she purred.

'I ain't bein' modest, ma'am, jest bein' honest.'

Her blue eyes widened. 'Honest and polite too, huh?'

He didn't know quite what to make of her approach.

'I'm Lou-Lou,' she introduced herself, though he felt it unnecessary. No other woman in Sundown saloon could outshine her.

'I'm Jay,' his deep, raw voice uttered his temporary identity.

'That's not yer real name though, is it?'

'No ma'am.'

She sat down at his table, her eyes raking into him with an intensity he'd never experienced from a woman. However, behind their blueness lurked something suspicious. 'Never met a man who was a stranger to himself,' she smiled alluringly.

'Won't be long before I remember,' Jay stated with assurance.

'What if ya don't?' she teased.

'I will.' He was adamant, and beginning to wonder what Lou-Lou's purpose was. His eyes stripped beneath the surface of her glittering façade trying to fathom the woman who hid behind it.

'I hear you're fast with a gun,' she surprised him.

He pounced on her words. 'Who told ya that?'

'Ain't no secrets in the Sundown, Jay. News travels fast here. I heard some fellers talkin' 'bout you and Corey Garrett practising target shootin' today.'

'Was one of them a Mexican by the name of Silvano?' Jay insisted she tell him.

'Might have been,' she toyed with him.

'Yes or not?' He demanded a straight answer — and she gave him one.

'He was a Mexican. I don't know his name.'

'Who else was with him?'

'Four others. I think one of them might have been your brother.'

'My brother?' Jay sounded incredulous.

'I cain't be certain, but he sure talked 'bout ya as if he knew ya real well. An' he looked kinda like you — his face just missed bein' handsome too,' she paused then added, 'an' I noticed he had green eyes, same as you have. Don't see many men with such green eyes.'

'Was he dressed all in black?' he persisted.

'Yeh, kinda suited him too, with him bein' tall and lean.'

'How old was he?'

'Maybe a couple of years younger than you are.'

'Did ya catch his name?'

81

'Nope, but he wanted me to do him a favour,' she revealed.

'What favour?' Jay's eagerness to put the pieces together made him sound abrasive.

'Take it easy there, feller,' she said, putting the brakes on his quick succession of questions.

'I need to know,' he stated calmly.

'I understand, but he never told me what he wanted, 'cause I said to him that I don't believe in doin' no one no favours,' she explained. 'Doin' someone a favour can git ya killed faster than a bullet.'

'Then why ya doin' me a favour by tellin' me all this?'

Lou-Lou rose from her seat, but spoke in confidence. 'Copperstone could do with a bit of excitement to liven it up from time to time. But them five men are dangerous. I been around men long enough to be able to recognize who's bad and who ain't — and them men is *real* bad.'

Jay reached up and clasped hold of

her wrist. 'Thanks for the warnin',
Lou-Lou,' he whispered huskily.

Lou-Lou twisted away from him.
'Don't go all soft on me, Jay,' she
smiled wryly. 'It'll ruin your tough-guy
image.'

With that remark, she sashayed back
upstairs, trailing her words behind her
like the gold satin ribbons flowing from
the bustle of her glistening gown.

★ ★ ★

That evening, back at the Mistral, Jay
had a heap of thinking to do.

Was it possible he had a brother? A
brother whose character was dangerous,
and who rode with Silvano? He was
in two minds what to think. Why
hadn't his brother approached him
in the mercantile? The man Lou-Lou
mentioned matched the description of
the stranger dressed in black who was
shadowed in the store's doorway.

And why was every darn thing
he did spread like wildfire around

Copperstone? For a man without an identity, he was sure getting one fast.

The last thing he needed was for folks to get the wrong impression. It was wrong, wasn't it? he asked himself. Sometimes, he felt as if he were clutching at straws, and sensed time was against him. If he wasn't careful, someone would surely get him while his memory was a blank. It would be like shooting him when his back was turned — he wouldn't stand a chance.

Lying in bed, he questioned everything that had happened to him in the past two days. Sleep eventually stole away the answers . . .

5

Lorn Catlin and his gang spent the evening in the Sundown saloon. Lou-Lou knew she should have ignored them, but curiosity got the better of her. So, when Lorn offered to buy her a drink, she took the opportunity to use her feminine wiles to find out what she wanted to know.

'Don't see many men with such attractive green eyes,' she flirted with him, accepting his offer of a drink.

Blind-sided by her flattery, Lorn dropped his guard. 'And I've never seen a woman with such wicked blue eyes,' he grinned.

She smiled. 'It must have been your brother who was in here earlier.' She threw her comment at him as sweetly as possible, while inwardly intent on gauging his reaction.

'My brother?'

'He had green eyes too, though he wasn't as handsome as you are,' she said, turning her lie into a flirtation.

Bedazzled by Lou-Lou, Lorn didn't realize he was being deliberately misled. 'I ain't got no brother, but my friends here, they're jest like family.'

'You're fairly new in town, ain't ya,' Lou-Lou purred. 'Where ya all from?'

'Oh, me an' the boys are jest passin' through,' he answered casually.

'The other feller, the one I took to be your brother, he's a stranger in town too,' she chatted brightly, determined to wring as much information out of him as possible. 'Maybe ya know him? Goes by the name of Jay.'

Mentioning Jay certainly caused an adverse reaction in Lorn. Judging by the twitching muscle in his cruel jaw, she'd hit a nerve, but he did his best to hide it.

The other four men sat drinking quietly, as if taking their lead from Lorn. However, she noted their eyes spark with recognition regarding Jay and caught the sly looks that passed between them all.

'Jay's not his real name though,' she continued, pretending to pass on local gossip. 'I hear he's lost his memory, and folks jest call him Jay.'

'Is that right?' Lorn was the one to start pretending. 'Well, whoever he is, he ain't no brother of mine,' he smiled broadly, holding Lou-Lou's gaze in an attempt to emphasize his honesty.

She knew it was time she made her exit from the gang's company before their suspicions were aroused. 'Guess it's time I left you boys to enjoy the rest of your evenin'. Thanks for the drink, feller,' she beamed at Lorn. 'No doubt I'll be seein' ya agin' at the Sundown.'

Lorn smiled, but didn't confirm her comment.

Before leaving, Lou-Lou asked as if it was an afterthought, 'I didn't catch your name, handsome.'

'My friends call me — Green,' he lied with a sly grin, having no intention of telling her who he was.

She wondered if he was lying. Certainly, he was smiling, but his smile failed to reach his cold green eyes. She also wondered what his enemies called him, but was wise enough to sense it would be dangerous to ask.

Flashing Lorn the brightest smile she could muster, Lou-Lou sashayed away.

Silvano, Roscoe, Sparks and Yerby the Kid all stared at Lorn.

'What ya lookin' at?'

'She's right, ya do look a bit like Jake Farr,' the Kid commented, noticing the resemblance for the first time.

'Same green eyes, dark hair and tall, lean build,' Sparks verified.

Silvano and Roscoe agreed unanimously.

Lorn took a long, hard look at himself in the saloon's large mirror, mentally comparing himself to Jake Farr. After several seconds, he laughed aloud. 'I'll be darned! I could pass for Jake's younger brother, couldn't I?' Still studying his reflection, he grinned, sly as a timber wolf. 'That's just given me an idea.'

★ ★ ★

Next day, Lorn and his gang rode out to the Mistral, bringing trouble in their wake.

The sun beat down relentlessly, as if it bore a special animosity and wished to burn the ground to a cinder — and them with it.

Stripped to the waist, Jay was working alone in the barn, unaware that the predatory horde had arrived. Meanwhile, Deakin, Bodine and Lucky were standing outside the bunkhouse drinking coffee when the gang rode up to them. The rest of the ranch-hands were away working the range with Chuck and Corey Garrett. Nobody else was around.

'We're lookin' fer a man called Jay,' Lorn announced bluntly.

Taking an instant dislike to Lorn,

Deakin sneered his reply, 'What d'ya want him fer?'

'Ain't no business of yours,' Silvano hissed.

Deakin's hackles rose. 'I weren't talkin' to you, *Mex*,' he mouthed in a derogatory way. 'But as charge-hand, everythin' on this ranch is my business.'

Sensing there was trouble brewing, Lucky tried to sidle off to his cookhouse.

'Where d'ya think you're goin', old-timer?' Lorn's voice halted Lucky in his tracks. 'You jest stay right where I can see ya.'

'But I got somethin' cookin' on the stove,' he lied, hoping to fetch his trusty scatter-gun in case things turned nasty. 'It'll burn.'

'Let it burn,' Lorn stated coldly.

Lucky stayed put. Beside him, Bodine stood stock-still, trying to make himself invisible. He was still recovering from the beating Jay had given him. Amber Lainey had told him he'd suffered a fractured clavicle. He wasn't sure what that meant, all he knew was his neck and shoulder throbbed with a dull ache, and he was in no fit state to get involved in another fight of Deakin's making.

'Jest who the hell d'ya think ya are?' Deakin snapped abrasively at Lorn, feeling safe on his own territory, and edging towards a rumble.

Lorn threw him a lethal glare. 'I'm the man who'll put a bullet in that smart mouth of yours if ya don't hurry up an' tell me where Jay is.'

Deakin stiffened. 'I don't like bein' threatened.'

Lorn's green eyes inched towards the pistol in his holster.

With lightning speed, Yerby the Kid drew his Colt .45 and pointed it straight at Deakin.

'I ain't afeared of no kid,' Deakin pronounced, making the same mistake numerous others had before him.

Lorn's tone was a warning whisper. 'This kid'll kill ya quicker than I will.'

It was the way Lorn said things that

made people believe him. And they were right to do so, because Lorn rarely bluffed when it came to killing.

Deakin refrained from any further attempt to draw his pistol. 'Jay's workin' in the barn,' he scowled, gesturing in its general direction.

'Keep an eye on 'em while we go check out the barn,' Lorn instructed Roscoe and Sparks.

The barn doors were wide open. 'There he is,' Silvano rasped, spying Jay inside. The three of them dismounted, tying the horses to a hitching post in the barnyard, and walked towards the entrance.

Hearing them approach, Jay turned to face them. In his right hand he held a lethal looking baling-hook which he was using to stack bales of hay for the horses' feed.

The heat inside the barn was ferocious, and sweat was pouring from Jay's brow, running rivulets into his eyes. He wiped it away with the back of his hand for a clearer look.

Bright sunlight streamed in from outside, causing Lorn, Silvano and the Kid to appear silhouetted against its fierce glow.

'Lookin' fer somethin?' Jay called out, trying to make out who was standing there watching him.

Lorn stepped forward into the darkness, making it easier for Jay to see exactly who he was. 'Lookin' fer you.'

Realization struck Jay like a hammer striking steel. In front of him was the man Lou-Lou said might be his own brother. With his green eyes, tall, lean frame and dark appearance, it was possible. However, something made him wary. A sense deep down in his gut. And unless he was mistaken, that was Silvano flanking him, along with a blond kid he'd never seen before.

'We hear ya ain't got no memory,' Lorn began.

'Who told ya?' returned Jay.

'A stranger like you gits noticed in

a small town,' Lorn replied. 'People round here like to know a man's name and his purpose — but even you don't know that, or do ya?'

'He don't know nothing,' emphasized Silvano. 'He don't even know his real name.'

Lorn intervened. 'Don't ya remember your name, Avery? Avery Catlin?'

Jay's mind didn't recognize the name. 'Who might you be?' he hedged.

Lorn smiled, wringing out his words for full impact. 'I'm Lorn Catlin — your brother. An' these boys here are your friends. That right, boys?'

A discord of emotions jolted through Jay, confusing him into silence.

'We've been a lookin' fer ya, Avery. Almost gave ya up fer dead,' said the Kid.

'Why didn't ya approach me in the mercantile?' Jay asked Lorn.

'When ya didn't turn up at the cabin, we reckoned ya might be dead. Then we heard a rumour about a feller, matchin' your description, who'd lost his memory. So, Silvano went in to see if it really was you.'

'He weren't none too friendly for somebody who's supposed to be my friend,' Jay commented astutely.

'I wasn't sure how ya'd react,' Silvano defended his actions. 'You always was unpredictable.'

Jay wasn't entirely convinced by Silvano's excuse.

'Ya have to remember,' Lorn emphasized, 'that we're wanted by the law. We had to be careful we weren't walkin' into some sorta trap. We took a chance comin' back into Copperstone to git ya.'

'Wanted by the law?' Jay picked up on Lorn's confession. 'What ya wanted fer?'

Lorn looked at him in mock surprise. 'We're outlaws, Avery — same as you.'

Jay was thunderstruck. In the space of a few moments, he'd learned he was Avery Catlin, an outlaw. Once again, his world was turned upside down.

'I can see all this is gonna take some

time to git used to,' Lorn faked his concern.

'Why should I believe you?' he gasped, his grip tightening on the bale-hook as the tension in his body mounted.

Lorn spread his arms wide. 'Why should we lie?' he said innocently.

'If we was gonna lie, we wouldn't have told ya we was outlaws,' the Kid reasoned.

'The Kid's right, Avery,' Lorn added persuasively. 'We're takin' a risk bein' here.'

Much as Jay hated to admit it to himself, what Lorn said made sense. It would certainly explain how he could fist-fight and shoot like his life depended on it. These were traits an outlaw would need to survive.

'Is it right that your memory will eventually return to normal?' Kid Yerby enquired.

Still deep in his own devastating thoughts, Jay nodded. Though he wasn't Jay any more. Jay had gone.

He was Avery now.

'Let's go, Brother,' Lorn beckoned.

'Go where?'

'Some place safe. We got a secure cabin a few miles away. We'll stay there a short while before headin' south like we planned.'

'I don't feel like a man who belongs to a pack,' Jay stated. 'I feel more like a loner.'

'Oh, ya always was a loner. We jest let ya be most of the time. But ya did ride with us, Avery,' Lorn assured him.

Gutted to the bone, the truth started to sink in.

'I cain't just walk away from the Mistral without givin' some sort a explanation to the Garretts. They gave me a month's wages in advance.'

Silvano laughed. 'Robbin' decent folks never bothered ya before.'

'We have to git outa here, Avery,' Lorn insisted. 'The longer ya stay, the more likely someone will recognize ya — and the law are already on yer trail.'

Feeling he had no other immediate choice, Jay decided to go with them. Later, at their cabin, he'd have time to think things through and figure out his next move.

Sinking the bale-hook into a stack of hay with as much pent-up force as he could expel, Jay followed them outside. Silvano inwardly flinched at the viciousness of his frustration, glad he wasn't on the receiving end of the hook's deadly spike.

The three outlaws mounted their horses and, with a heavy heart, Jay rode the mustang Corey Garrett had loaned him. He also strapped on the Smith and Wesson which he'd hung at the barn door.

Sparks and Roscoe were still holding their captives at gun point.

'What's goin' on?' Jay questioned the situation, particularly annoyed that old Lucky was being threatened.

'It was Deakin's fault,' Bodine distanced himself from any blame. 'He spoke outa turn — '

'Shut up,' Roscoe's gaunt face snarled at Bodine, frightening him into silence.

'This here's Sparks Becker and Roscoe Nash,' Lorn informed Jay. 'I know ya don't remember 'em, or Yerby the Kid here, but we're the only real friends ya got.'

'Ya low-down varmint,' Deakin spat at Jay, which only proved to strengthen Lorn's claim. 'I knew ya was no good the first time I clapped eyes on ya. Me and Bodine should've killed ya when we had the chance.'

Lorn's face turned into a deathly cold mask. 'Nobody talks to my brother like that — and lives.' Instantly, he drew his Colt and targeted Deakin.

Jay put a hand up to stop him firing. 'He ain't worth killin'.'

For several pulsing seconds, Lorn weighed up the options, before withdrawing his Colt. His eyes narrowed into green slits. 'Go git your belongings from the bunkhouse, then we'll be on our way.'

Sliding off the mustang, Jay did as

Lorn suggested, quickly collecting his personal belongings and tying them on to his horse's saddle. Remounting, his eyes met the disbelief of Lucky's face, and although he felt the urge to go against the grain of the outlaws, he feared the wrath of the law. For some unknown reason, he'd chosen to live on the dark side of life, and there was no easy way back. Maybe when he could remember his past, he'd understand why he'd become an outlaw. And if he was real fortunate, he might be able to deal himself a more honest hand than the dirty game he was being forced to play right now.

'Ya won't git away with this,' Deakin threatened Jay directly as the outlaws made to leave. 'I'll make sure the law gits ya — and yer sly-eyed brother.'

With those words, Deakin sealed his fate. If he'd kept his mouth shut, the outlaws would have left without doing them any real harm. One wrong move was all it took to change the outcome.

Without hesitation, Lorn drew his Colt.

Bodine dived for cover as Lorn shot Deakin clean through the skull — silencing him forever. His lifeless body was thrown backwards with the force of the shot and landed in the water trough, turning the water crimson red.

Brave, but foolish, Lucky made a dash for the cookhouse to get his scatter-gun. Jay shouted a warning to Lucky, but he didn't heed it and continued to run towards the cookhouse door, making himself an easy prey for Silvano.

'Let the old man go,' Jay shouted.

Ignoring Jay's plea, Silvano aimed a deadly shot at Lucky's retreating figure. Acting on impulse, Jay nudged his mustang against Silvano's pinto, causing the shot to fire off-target, doing no more damage than graze the old man's shoulder, though it was enough to make him drop to the ground, writhing in pain.

'Let's git outa here, fast!' Lorn commanded.

Nobody, including Jay, needed telling twice. Spurring their horses to a gallop, they rode off the Mistral land without a backward glance.

Silvano didn't verbally make any comment to Jay about him trying to help Lucky, but his jet-black eyes spoke their displeasure loud and clear. Lorn, on the other hand, spoke his mind plainly.

'You're gonna have to decide what side you're on, Brother. Given the chance, that old fool would've shot any of us.'

It was true. Jay knew Lorn spoke the truth. However, it stuck in his throat to imagine standing by and letting Silvano gun down Lucky. He just didn't seem to have it in him to do that. Yet, one thing bothered him deeply: he didn't care about what happened to Deakin. On that, he had no feeling whatsoever. And this is what troubled him for the rest of the journey to the cabin.

Now and then, he'd cast a glance at Lorn as they rode side by side, wondering if he really was his brother. Wondering too, if he himself was an equally cold-hearted killer.

★ ★ ★

Verity Garrett came rushing from the ranchhouse, hearing the shots and fearing the worst. She'd been baking bread in the kitchen and wiped the surplus flour from her hands on to the blue gingham apron tied around her waist as she ran towards the bunkhouse.

One look at Deakin's body floating in the trough confirmed her fears, but her main concern was with the living.

Shaking from head to toe, Bodine was trying to help Lucky struggle to his feet. Verity gave him a hand and together they supported Lucky and got him into the bunkhouse.

'What happened?' she asked, strain etched across her face.

'Jay's an outlaw. His brother and four others, one of them a Mexican, came lookin' fer him,' Bodine explained bluntly. 'Deakin challenged them and ended up with a bullet between the eyes.' He glanced at the old man. 'And as fer Lucky, well, he sure was this time.'

Verity was genuinely astonished. 'I cain't believe Jay would condone this. I'd never have taken him fer bein' an outlaw.'

'It jest don't make no sense,' Lucky murmured as Verity tended his wound. 'Jay even tried to warn me that the Mexican was gonna shoot me.'

Bodine described what happened. 'Jay rammed his mustang into the Mexican's pinto, knockin' him off target. That's how come he missed killin' ya.'

'Fer that, I'm grateful to Jay,' Lucky admitted with relief.

Verity reinforced her astonishment. 'I cain't hardly believe this has happened. When I tell Chuck and Corey, they'll be reelin' mad for givin' Jay a chance and then he goes and suckers us for a month's money and steals the mustang into the bargin.'

'Want me to go git Chuck and Corey?' Bodine offered.

'I'll go git them, ya ain't fit enough yet to ride,' Verity sighed, feeling close to tears, seeing her flour-dusted apron now stained scarlet from the senseless violence which had shattered the peaceful existence of her beloved Mistral.

6

A languid breeze had sprung up from the river, but it barely cooled the hot sultry air, or the over-heated feelings of the townsfolk.

Panic gripped the town as word spread like wildfire that a murderous outlaw gang was on the loose in Copperstone.

With the sheriff out of town on court business, it was up to the local deputy, Abe McCoy, to take charge. Young and inexperienced, McCoy's only suggestion was to call a meeting.

The rooftop bell rang out in Copperstone's white-painted meeting-house, where everyone was summoned to hear McCoy's advice. The advice was short and simple. He told folks to stay calm and keep out of trouble. Someone had suggested they round up a posse, but this was vetoed by McCoy who said they shouldn't think of taking the law into their own hands. He reckoned the gang wouldn't risk coming back into Copperstone and were probably miles away by now. He also said he'd wired the sheriff, and that the sheriff had informed the US Marshal's office of the incident.

After the meeting disbanded, folks went on about their business, but in the back of their minds, they were watching and waiting for more signs of trouble.

Amber and Doc Lainey were approached by Lou-Lou as they left the meeting.

'I hear Lucky was shot. Is he gonna be all right?' There was genuine concern in Lou-Lou's question.

'He's gonna be fine,' Doc Lainey assured her. 'He got hit in the shoulder, but accordin' to Verity Garrett, it's just a flesh wound and she's attendin' to him.'

'The old fool,' Lou-Lou sighed, exasperated. 'Could have gotten himself killed.' Although he riled her at the best of times, she couldn't help liking him as he reminded her of the father she had lost some years back.

Deputy McCoy waylaid Doc Lainey, leaving the two young women to acquaint themselves. There was an initial awkwardness between them, for although they vaguely knew who the other was, neither of them had spoken or acknowledged each other properly before.

Amber had never really seen Lou-Lou up close. Being a lady, she didn't frequent the Sundown saloon. However, Amber had heard that men were instantly smitten with her, so she was naturally curious to study her in person. In the daylight, Amber thought Lou-Lou's spangled gown was garish and her lipstick bright as fire, but she could understand how some men would be attracted to such displays of brazenness. In comparison, Amber felt almost plain in her pretty blue dress and bonnet.

Simultaneously, Lou-Lou was studying Amber, thinking how naturally beautiful she was, and trying to remember if there was ever a time in her own life when she'd been so pure.

'It's dreadful that such violence has come to Copperstone,' Amber broke the silence with an innocuous statement. 'No one will be able to sleep safely in their beds at night until these murderers are caught.'

'I jest cain't believe that Jay's an outlaw,' Lou-Lou remarked, unable to contain her astonishment. 'I took him to be a decent sort.'

Amber's topaz eyes widened in surprise. 'You know Jay?'

'Met him in the Sundown,' Lou-Lou replied.

Amber's lips pursed disapprovingly. 'What was he doing there?'

Lou-Lou eyed her wryly. 'Same as any other man — havin' a drink and easin' the load of worries on his mind.'

'He confided in you?' Amber sounded incredulous.

'Don't sound so surprised, honey. I may not be your sort of woman, but I'm still a good listener.'

'What did Jay tell you?'

Lou-Lou was beginning to cotton on to Amber's drift. Obviously, she was sweet on Jay and jealous that he'd spent time in the company of a saloon girl. 'Nothin' much.'

'He must have said more than that,' Amber insisted disdainfully.

'What he said is between him and me,' Lou-Lou said, putting her firmly in her place.

'If you're tryin' to insinuate that Jay and you . . . ' Amber couldn't find the words to express herself politely.

'That Jay and I . . . went *upstairs* together,' Lou-Lou smilingly supplied the words for her.

'I'm not a prude,' Amber said, feeling the need to defend her attitude, 'neither am I a Jezebel. I simply want to know what Jay means to you.'

Lou-Lou swallowed the Jezebel insult in one resigned gulp, for although she would wish otherwise, that's exactly what she was. 'Listen, honey, I can tell you're sweet on Jay, so I'll put your mind at ease. Nothin' happened between us that ya couldn't show at one of your Sunday school meetings.'

Amber blushed. 'I never once said I was sweet on Jay — '

Lou-Lou cut her short. 'Ya didn't need to say, I can tell. It's written all over ya.'

Amber made to deny her feelings, but Lou-Lou's blue eyes told her to hush up. 'I ain't gonna tell nobody if that's what you're thinkin'.'

'D'ya really believe it's possible that Jay's an outlaw?' Amber's eyes pleaded for another woman's opinion.

'Nope, but everything points to the fact that he is.'

Solemnly, Amber nodded.

'Git yourself a good feller. Don't pin your dreams to a bad 'un,' Lou-Lou advised. 'I know what I'm talkin' 'bout. I let all the good ones slip through my fingers — and fell for all the wrong ones. A bad guy might seem more excitin', but ya'll never have a happy life together, believe me.'

Amber did believe her. 'I'm sorry I called you a Jezebel,' she apologized, seeing Lou-Lou in a kinder light.

'Forgit it,' said Lou-Lou.

'Amber!' Corey Garrett's voice interrupted the women's conversation. 'I've jest been speakin' to your father. It's so awful to think we've both harboured an outlaw under our roof.'

Although Corey was intimately acquainted with Lou-Lou, he completely ignored her and spoke only to Amber.

Knowing this was her cue to leave them alone, Lou-Lou cast Amber a tell-tale look before walking away. It was an expression that warned Amber to beware of trusting Corey Garrett, at least in a romantic sense. Amber took the warning to heart, intending not to allow herself to be fooled by him. She blinked her acknowledgement to Lou-Lou.

It was common knowledge that

Corey planned one day to ask Amber to marry him. Their courting had been entirely innocent, mainly because Amber kept Corey at a safe distance. With few suitable young unmarried men in Copperstone she seemed almost resigned to the inevitable — that she would indeed agree to become his wife, despite feeling no great passion or intense love for him. Now, she would think twice before giving in so easily. For months she'd heard rumours that Corey regularly visited the Sundown and that he was secretly smitten with Lou-Lou. Up until today, she'd dismissed it as being nothing more than idle gossip. The look on Lou-Lou's face had changed her mind.

★ ★ ★

Hidden by a dense forest of juniper trees, the outlaw's cabin was indeed a safe hideaway. Sparsely furnished, it was sufficient for their basic needs. It belonged to a cousin of Sparks Becker

113

who was currently in a Texas jail.

Sparks fixed them all something to eat, while Yarby the Kid and Roscoe tended to the horses. Meanwhile, Lorn and Silvano were huddled in a far corner of the cabin, deep in secretive discussion. Jay couldn't hear what they were saying, but he surmised they were deciding what to do about him. And he hoped they would come up with some good suggestions on how to help him remember everything he'd forgotten.

Jay watched the stoutly solid figure of Sparks as he busied himself at the stove, inwardly perplexed that he had no recollection of ever having seen his snub-nosed, squashed-featured face ever before. The same non-recognition applied to slat-thin Roscoe. These two men were a total blank to him.

As for the other three, he felt he knew them — distantly. Silvano and Lorn were vaguely familiar, although the blond Kid was less so. In particular, there was something about Silvano and the Kid that sent a cold shiver through his blood. The skeleton on Silvano's sleeve, he was sure, was a constant trigger to opening the door to his past. He just couldn't quite reach it — yet.

His brother, Lorn was a relative stranger. Whenever he looked into Lorn's green eyes, he saw himself reflected. And, to be honest, he didn't like what he saw.

* * *

'Now we got Jake Farr, what d'ya plan on doin' next?' Silvano asked Lorn in a whispered rasp.

'I got it all figured out,' Lorn cast him a conceited grin. 'I say we git him to rob the bank at Redville.'

'But we was gonna do it ourselves,' said Silvano, puzzled. 'That's why we're here in Copperstone.'

Redville was ten miles from Copperstone, and the gang's original plan was to use the cabin as a safe base from which to rob the bank at Redville.

'I know what we planned, but now

115

we can use Jake to rob the bank. Let him take the risk of gittin' caught by the law, while we wait here.'

'Could he do it? After all, he's never robbed a bank before.'

'I'll bet he'll make a better job of it than us,' Lorn stated confidently. 'Jake's smart, he's fast with a gun and he sure can handle himself in a fight. All things considered, Jake would've made one hell of an outlaw.'

Silvano smiled. The idea really appealed to him. 'There's only one problem,' he pointed out. 'How ya gonna git Jake to go along with the plan?'

'I'm gonna tell him we need the money so all of us can start a new life in Mexico. I'll explain that we cain't do the robbery 'cause we're wanted in Redville, an' he's the only one among the six of us who isn't wanted there. And, before he lost his memory, he promised to do this one last job for us.'

'An' if he refuses?'

'Then I'll kill him,' Lorn shrugged, without a shred of emotion. 'It's as simple as that.'

An anxious thought crossed Silvano's mind. 'What if he starts rememberin' the truth?'

With a slow shake of his head, Lorn dismissed such a worry. 'Ya seen the blank way he looks at us. He ain't gonna remember much for a long while yet. By the time he finds out who he really is, he'll have already discredited himself and will never be a threat to any of us ever again.'

'So, we git rich from the money he steals, *and* we git him off our backs for good,' Silvano summarized.

'That's right.'

'How d'ya think up such twisted ideas?' There was a compliment in Silvano's voice.

''Cause I'm a born criminal,' he grinned wryly.

Silvano's crooked teeth formed into a lop-sided smirk. 'What will we do with him after we've got the money?'

'Finish off what we tried to do to him before — only this time, we'll do it right.'

'He's mine.' Silvano savoured the pleasure of killing Jake.

'I said,' Lorn emphasized, 'this time we'll do it right. Ya shot him once before and didn't even put a dent in him.'

'The bullet hit his gold pocket watch.'

'I don't want no excuses. I heard your excuses too many times, Silvano. You and Kid Yerby also assured me Jake was dead when ya both left him lying near Copperstone's river. That's twice ya failed to kill him.'

'He would have died eventually, if that boy hadn't fetched the doc.'

'But he didn't die, did he?' Lorn's teeth were gritted so hard, it almost seemed like he was snarling.

Silvano didn't press the point. He knew when to draw the line in an argument with Lorn.

'If yer wantin' fed,' Sparks announced

to anyone listening, 'better come and git it.'

Roscoe and the Kid walked in in time to hear that the food was ready and made a bee-line for the kitchen where Sparks had unceremoniously laid six plates, a pot of beef stew and a pan of beans for everyone.

Sitting round the table, the six men ate first and talked later, drinking a whole pot of rich, strong coffee between them.

Chewing on a plug of tobacco, Lorn was about to bring up the subject of the Redville robbery when a single crack of gunshot sounded outside in the distance.

'Reckon they rounded up a posse to find us?' Roscoe murmured ominously.

'Could be nothin',' Lorn reasoned.

'I'll go see,' Silvano volunteered. 'If I ain't back soon . . . '

Lorn nodded. 'We'll come lookin' fer ya.'

'I'll go with ya,' said Kid Yerby.

Stealthily, Silvano and the Kid

ventured out into the twilight on foot. Night was falling fast and they welcomed its haste. Merging with the shadows of the thick juniper trees, Jay and Lorn watched them disappear into the surrounding forest.

Meanwhile, Roscoe and Sparks saddled up the horses in case the gang needed to make a quick getaway.

Inside, Jay and Lorn stood side by side at the windows, gun at the ready to defend the cabin if need be. Jay was impressed at how cool Lorn was under pressure, calmly chewing on his plug of tobacco as he checked the load and action of his Winchester.

Lorn read the unspoken thoughts which were clearly etched across Jay's strong-boned face. 'We been in tighter corners than this, Brother, and the law ain't caught us yet.'

The sweet scent of the tobacco's molasses casing on Lorn's breath reminded Jay of the past. Vaguely he remembered a blurred figure dressed in black, holding a pistol at close range — and laughing. His laughter was laced with the distinctive scent of molasses. The memory gave Jay a deep sense of foreboding which he couldn't quite fathom, but this was neither the time or the place to rack his brains for memories. He had to keep his wits alert and his eyes focused sharply on the impending threat.

★ ★ ★

The sound of men's voices raised in argument led Silvano and the Kid to the edge of the forest where several riders were grouped in a clearing. Hidden by the thick guard of trees, the outlaws watched and listened to them quarrel.

Silvano recognized some of them. Among then was Corey and Chuck Garrett, young Deputy Abe McCoy and a few nameless faces from Copperstone, including the mercantile store-keeper and the blacksmith.

Corey and McCoy were opposed to Chuck Garrett and the others who had formed an unauthorized posse to track down and kill or capture the outlaws. The two of them had ridden after the posse to stop them, catching up with them at the clearing, having also heard the gunshot.

'Those outlaws ain't gonna git away with shootin' my ranch-hands, stealin' my mustang and suckerin' me for money,' Chuck wrangled.

Corey wasn't on his father's side. In fact, it was Corey who had alerted the deputy when he realized his father and five other men were hell-bent on riding after the outlaws. He didn't want to see his father get hurt, neither did he want him to take the law into his own hands.

'I'm orderin' ya all to turn around an' head back into town real peaceful like,' McCoy tried to reason with them. 'I cain't have a posse runnin' loose in these parts and shootin' wild.'

'I aimed high,' Chuck argued, obviously having been the one who fired the stray shot. 'Thought I saw that Jay character skulking in the shadows.'

'There ain't nobody but us,' stated Corey. 'An' if there was, it could've been an innocent man. It's too darn dark to be shootin' at shadows!'

'We cain't jest stand back an' let them varmints escape,' Hal Wallace, the mercantile store-keeper, protested. 'I got a good look at Jay and that Mexican feller when they was in my store. I'd know 'em agin if I ever saw 'em, even in the dark.'

McCoy stood firm against the unruly posse. 'Yer all fired-up an' not thinkin' straight. Let the law handle this.'

'No offence, Abe,' said Chuck, 'but a young slip of a boy like you ain't up to a man's job. If Sheriff Doby had been here, he'd have rounded up a posse and gone right after them outlaws.'

'I told ya at the meeting that the sheriff was dead against anythin' like this,' McCoy shouted in frustration.

'Come home, Pa,' said Corey, trying to make his father see sense. 'Ma's sick with worry. Let it be. Them outlaws are long gone by now anyways.'

'It's no use, Corey, I made up my mind to do this.' Chuck refused to be moved and any hint of surrender on his life-weary face closed with the finality of a door slamming.

'If them outlaws are anywhere near here, we'll find 'em and see that justice is done,' Hal Wallace muttered in vengeance, gripping his shot-gun defiantly.

Barely had these words filtered into the dusky night air, than Wallace was catapulted off his roan by the force of Kid Yarby's bullet, which ploughed into his throat, undamming a torrent of blood and effectively silencing him forever.

The posse scattered in a blind panic, trying to control their jittered horses and defend themselves against the unseen attackers, by firing chaotically into the darkness.

Without mercy, the outlaws cut them down in a ruthless hail of lead. Bullets flashed through the moonlit blackness like deadly fireflies, and the scent of gunsmoke singed the starless night sky.

Within seconds, Silvano shot Deputy McCoy, bursting his youthful heart wide open. His chest gushed crimson and, dead on impact, he fell to the ground without a murmur.

The town's blacksmith, Jethro Samuels, a large, burly man, cried out in horror and was instantly killed by the trio of bullets Kid Yerby pumped into his rotund torso.

Unprepared for such savagery, the posse was overpowered by the ferocity of the outlaws' devastating onslaught.

Corey couldn't breathe, he couldn't think and, just for a moment, he couldn't see anything except a black void.

Two Colts blazing fire and smoke; Kid Yarby ruthlessly shot a retreating posse man in the back as he attempted a hasty escape. The dying rider gurgled a mouthful of hot blood and tumbled from the side of his saddle. To add to the man's agony, his foot got entangled and trapped by the reins, and his spooked horse galloped off at speed, dragging his body along the rough ground in the minutes it took him to finally die.

Silvano shot and killed two others and wounded a third — Chuck Garrett. Spitting blood, Chuck found the strength to keep himself in the saddle and ride off, flanked by Corey. Father and son were the only ones to escape alive.

7

'Chuck's hurt real bad,' Doc Lainey informed Verity.

She glanced with red-rimmed eyes at Corey as Chuck lay in the care of Doc Lainey and Amber. Corey had managed to get his father to the Laineys' house, but was himself still in a state of shock.

'Will he pull through?' Verity's voice trembled, clutching her husband's limp hand as he lay unconscious on the bed.

'He's a fighter, ain't he?' said the doc, trying to rally her spirits.

Verity nodded solemnly, thinking to herself that it was because he was a fighter he'd got himself shot.

Doc Lainey pulled Corey aside while Amber comforted Verity and kept a vigil at Chuck's bedside.

'You certain the others are dead?'

the doc was compelled to ask.

'Pa and I were the only ones who made it,' he stammered, shivering with delayed shock. 'Abe, Hal, Jethro and the others never had a chance against them outlaws.'

'Did ya git a good look at 'em? Was Jay there?'

'Nope, but it must've been them. Who else would open fire like that and gun us down in cold blood?'

Voices seeped into the house from outside as word of the massacre broke through the sleeping town.

'Go tell 'em I'll be out in a minute,' the doc instructed Derry.

The young boy did as he was bid.

Doc Lainey stepped out on to the front porch to face the crowd of anxious townsfolk who'd gathered there. His voice throbbed with emotion as he spoke the names of the men who'd died. In the moment of crisis, everyone rallied round, comforting those families who had lost someone dear to them, mourning too, the friends they would themselves miss.

'With Abe gone, someone will have to telegraph Sheriff Dolby and tell him we need help — fast,' the doc announced.

The town clerk spoke up. 'I'll go do that right away,' he confirmed, hurrying off.

'In the meantime,' the doc continued, 'I suggest we all keep a vigilant eye open for these outlaws in case they decide to come back into Copperstone. It's doubtful they'll risk it, but don't take no chances. Any strangers comin' into town will have to prove who they are and what their business is, until we know the outlaws are long gone.'

'Maybe we should git some volunteers to step into the shoes of Abe and Sheriff Dolby,' Corey suggested to them. He then stepped towards the crowd of distressed faces. 'I'll volunteer myself.'

Without hesitation, more than a dozen men followed his example, each man ready and willing to do his duty to protect Copperstone.

'I know I'm an old-timer,' Eben Stanley, who helped out at the town bakery admitted, 'but I was a deputy in Wyoming in my younger days, and I'd sure be willin' to volunteer if ya'll have me.'

'Thanks, Eben,' declared Corey. 'We need a man like you.'

Eben was pleased, and had a couple of immediate ideas to put to the others. 'I'd like to suggest we work shifts in the sheriff's office, in groups of five, and always have someone keepin' a lookout from the meeting-house bell-tower. At the first sign of trouble, they'd ring the bell to warn us all. An' at night, we keep the town well lit so whoever is on watch in the tower can see what's goin' on.'

Eben's ideas met with everyone's approval, and five men grouped together, stating they'd form the first shift. Corey added that he'd stand lookout in the tower.

'Go home now an' git some sleep,'

the doc advised, effectively dispersing the crowd.

* * *

Meanwhile, Jay and Lorn had waited patiently, listening to the gunfire, then listening it to it cease.

Jay couldn't decide which was worse — the sound or the silence — but either way, he was secretly steeling himself for the approach of the posse.

Outside, Roscoe and Sparks were on tenterhooks, guarding the rear of the cabin, and ensuring the horses weren't spooked.

In stark contrast, Lorn remained as calm as a marble statue, his eyes frozen into watchful stillness.

'Silvano and the kid can look after themselves in a gunfight,' Lorn stated without a shadow of a doubt. 'Just hang tight. They'll be back soon, then we'll decide where we go from here.'

Where would they go from here? Jay pondered, feeling trapped in a limbo of darkness. He also pondered deeply over the Redville robbery. Minutes earlier, Lorn had explained to Jay about the plan to rob the bank at Redville, and his mind was trying to reconcile itself to the possibility of this lawless task. According to his brother, he'd already promised to do this one last job for them.

Initially, Jay refused to comply, but Lorn persisted, using all his powers of persuasion and guile to sway him. Lorn promised that nobody would get hurt. All Jay had to do was steal the money. The plan was foolproof, and once they had the money, they could all put the past behind them and begin a new life.

Although reluctant to go along with such a plan, Jay felt this might be the only way for them to make a clean break from their life of crime, and start afresh in Mexico. He didn't want to be on the run from the law indefinitely, forever looking over his shoulder for a man with a badge. Neither did he want to live a pauper's existence in Mexico, for this would inevitably lead him and his brother into further crime. For these reasons, he said he'd think it over. Lorn told him he had until morning to make up his mind.

Jay admired his brother's confidence that they'd survive until morning, especially with a posse hounding them down.

'We might have to head for Redville tonight,' Lorn declared, disturbing Jay's pensive thoughts.

'I thought you and the others were wanted there?' Jay pounced on his contradictory words. 'Surely that's why ya asked me to rob the bank while you all stayed put?'

Lorn had some quick thinking to do. Jake was astute and not easy to fool. 'Oh we *are* wanted in Redville, but that was a long time ago. Chances are, the lawmen there won't remember us, that's if they're still alive. Lawmen in Redville don't have a long life expectancy. It's a raw railroad town full of hardcases. Too many men like us are there already. We'll blend right into the crowd, especially if we ride in separately or in pairs.'

'In that case, you can help me rob the bank,' Jay stated forcefully.

'Ya decided to do it?' Lorn grinned.

'Cain't see as I got much choice. It's not like we'll be killin' nobody, jest relievin' 'em of their money,' Jay said, trying to convince himself more than convince Lorn.

'That's right, Avery. An' when we got the money, we can find our freedom across the border.'

'An' no more killin'?' Jay wanted a guarantee.

'Ya have my word,' Lorn lied, through a smile of sly cunning.

For a long moment, Jay studied Lorn's profile. Chiselled sharp, his face reflected a strange determination, as if he had forbidden himself to express fear. Shuttered behind his eyes, which side on appeared to be transparent green glass, was a hidden reason for his cruel lifestyle. Something buried deep down long ago. Something which compelled him to dress from head to toe in black, including a black leather holster. Jay wondered what Lorn's secret was, because maybe it was the key to his own lawless situation.

'How did you an' I git ourselves involved in a life like this?' Jay asked. 'Ain't we got no family to consider?'

Two slivers of green glass looked directly at him in reply. 'They're all dead.'

Jay swallowed the bad news with a heavy heart. 'What happened?' His deep voice was laced with solemnity.

'When we were kids, we lived on a ranch in Arizona. One day, Ma and Pa were gunned down right in front of our eyes. Nobody cared. The murderers got clean away. An' you and me, Avery, brought ourselves up the hard way. I was ten and you wasn't much older. We had to grow up real fast.'

'I don't remember,' Jay admitted, almost in apology for not being able to recall something so poignant.

'Best ya don't,' Lorn stated tonelessly.

Moments later, Silvano and Kid Yerby burst into the cabin, relaying everything that had happened.

Lorn's first thoughts regarded their own survival. 'This hideout ain't safe no more. If the Garretts got away, they'll alert the townsfolk and we could have another posse on its way,' Lorn reasoned. 'We're gonna have to head for Redville. If we leave now, we'll be there by dawn.'

Jay's first thoughts concerned those who'd died. 'Did ya have to kill 'em?' His voice was a coiled spring of anger barely kept in check.

Silvano iced Jay with a steely glare. 'They was hell-bent on killin' us,' he rasped, the scar across his cheekbone drawn tight with pent-up fury.

It was inevitable that Jay and Silvano should spark each other up the wrong way. Dominant males usually did.

'Silvano's right,' Kid Yerby echoed. 'The posse was scouring the area and would've shot us given half a chance. The deputy was urgin' them to turn around and go back home, but they was havin' none of it. We didn't have no choice, Avery.'

Tight-lipped, Jay nodded his understanding, though his guts were twisting in sympathy for the good men who'd died fighting for their own sense of justice.

'Gather your belongings and let's git goin',' Lorn commanded.

Without further discussion, they all gathered their few possessions. Jay's consisted of a leather bag given to him by Doc Lainey, together with his new clothes from the mercantile rolled up and tied tight. The others travelled similarly light.

In the moments it took Jay to gather his things, he felt Silvano following him with eyes of jet, his lips tense with disapproval at his presence. Jay retaliated with a glare that burned a fierce green fire. Silvano read Jay's meaning loud and clear. Their day of reckoning was coming. It was a warning — with a promise.

Outside, they mounted up and picked their way through the thick forest whose trees looked like an army of ghosts standing shoulder to shoulder against the blackness. The sky was heavy, dark-hearted and silent. Jay thought how closely it reflected his own spirits. Come dawn, all that had happened this evening would vanish like a ghoulish nightmare, leaving only the unsettling aftermath that would gradually disappear in the daylight.

The light at the end of Jay's tunnel, however, seemed a long way off. He wasn't quite sure what lay ahead at Redville, but whatever it was, he sensed it wouldn't be pleasant.

★ ★ ★

Redville was teeming with trouble. It was a tough place brimming with everyone from rough railroad men to cardsharps and general hardcases.

138

Next morning, when Jay and the outlaws rode in, they hardly altered the waterline. Like a bucketful of water, a few more drops made no noticeable difference.

Although it really wasn't necessary, they'd split into three pairs to make themselves less conspicuous; Lorn and Jay, Silvano and Kid Yerby, and Sparks and Roscoe. Each pair stayed in separate rooms, but at the same hotel. The hotel they chose was directly opposite the bank. It was a deliberate choice. Proximity was an advantage, allowing the outlaws to watch the bank from the bedroom windows of the Red Hot Poker Hotel. Lorn had it all figured out, right down to the last detail.

'We'll stay here for a few days, jest to make sure they ain't changed their policy at the bank,' Lorn explained to Jay.

'What policy would that be?'

'At the beginning of the month, the railroad men's wages are brought into Redville by armed stagecoach from the rail company's headquarters. The money is put in the bank, and lies there overnight before being collected the next day and distributed to the workers.'

'So, unless they do things differently, the money we're after is the railroad wages?' Jay summarized.

'Yep. An' any other money in the safe that we can git out hands on while we're in there is a bonus,' Lorn confirmed, relishing the thought of all that cash.

'How we gonna git it?'

'From the banker, Owen Wexler. You're gonna force him to open the safe.'

Jay looked at Lorn aghast. 'How in heck's name am I gonna do that? What if he refuses?'

'Oh, Wexler won't refuse,' Lorn said, with sly certainty.

'What makes ya so sure?'

' 'Cause he's gittin' a share of whatever we steal.'

'I don't think I understand.'

'Course ya do,' Lorn smiled coldly. 'The banker's the biggest crook in town. I done a deal with him six months ago. It's all agreed. We pretend to force him at gunpoint to open the safe, then make off with the money. We tie him up before we leave so everyone believes it weren't his fault, and stash his share under the porch of his house.'

'It seems too easy.'

Lorn's expression of cold good-humour didn't waver. 'Nothin' in this life is ever easy, Avery. It took me months to plan this. An' we still gotta get away without anyone in town seein' us and gittin' suspicious.'

Jay's lean, strong face became thoughtful. 'Can we trust the banker?'

'Nope. Never trust nobody except yourself — and me of course,' Lorn added as an afterthought. 'You and me is blood, and that's different.'

'How d'ya git in tow with this crooked banker?'

'Just lucky I guess,' he joked.

'Seriously though, the world is full of decent-livin' outlaws; folks who'll sell ya down the river while pretendin' to be upright citizens. To my mind, they're far worse than outlaws like us. At least with us ya know what you're dealing with. We are what we are. But frauds like Wexler cheat ya all the way down the line.'

Jay ingested everything carefully, his mind searching for loopholes.

'We'll talk to Wexler tonight. Roscoe and Sparks have gone over to the bank to tell him we're here,' Lorn embellished.

'If your plan works, are ya really gonna give Wexler his share of the money?' Jay sounded doubtful, expecting Lorn to double-cross the banker.

'He'll git his share as agreed. That way, it sorta guarantees he'll keep his mouth shut.'

'Ain't no such thing as a sure-fire guarantee,' Jay seemed wise enough to know.

Lorn's expression rearranged into a

mask of viciousness. 'I'll give ya one.
If Wexler crosses me, I'll come back
an' kill him if it's the last thing I
ever do.'

Jay saw the killer glint in Lorn's eyes.
It was guarantee enough.

8

Manhunter, Kel Lobart rode slow and easy down the main street of Copperstone, unaware that the town's bell was ringing out a warning of his arrival. The signal caused a rush of panic to ripple through the townsfolk, clearing the street of women and children.

Lobart bore a hunter's face, devoid of weakness or pity. Though steel-grey eyes he watched the scenario warily, though he didn't falter from his purpose and continued towards the Sundown saloon.

A dozen unofficial deputies appeared as if from nowhere to challenge the unknown rider, an impressive figure who sat high in the saddle of his silver-maned palomino. The rider's hair was of similar colour and description. Prematurely grey for a man barely thirty, the stranger's silver locks were tied back into a pony-tail by a thin strip of leather underneath his grey, low-crowned stetson. Long, lithe and strong, Lobart was one of those men who would stay whipcord lean until the day he died, never giving age a chance to alter his physique.

Several shot-guns and pistols faced him as he approached the front of the Sundown.

'Expectin' trouble, boys?' the stranger's heavy voice levelled at them as he reined his horse to a halt.

'Who are ya?' Corey Garrett challenged, a Winchester in his determined grasp. 'An' what's yer purpose in Copperstone?'

'The name's Kel Lobart. I'm a manhunter from Montana, just passin' through.'

The faces behind the guns looked at him warily. He could see they weren't sure whether to believe him or not. He'd seen townsfolk frightened this way before. Simple, law-abiding people, forced by circumstance to defend their territory from newcomers. Usually, they'd recently tasted trouble from outlaws and weren't prepared to accept further torment.

Lobart's leather-gloved hand reached into the pocket of his grey duster coat and produced the necessary papers to verify his word.

'Who ya huntin'?' Corey asked, his eyes searching the papers for authenticity before passing them around the others.

'Huntin' the Catlin gang, and searching for a good friend of mine — Jake Farr.'

'We never heard of no Jake Farr,' Corey was cautious.

'I cain't be sure he came through Copperstone. We split up, arrangin' to meet later on. I went east and Jake rode this way, headin' for a railroad town by the name of Redville.'

'Redville's half a day's ride from here,' Corey told him.

'I'd like to rest awhile, then be on my way there. That's if you folks ain't got no objections.'

Lobart toted an ivory-handled Colt in a tied-down holster and a rifle in the saddle boot. Old Eben Stanley eyed the guns warily. 'Yer welcome here if ya ain't gonna start no trouble.'

There was an impressiveness about Lobart. An unaggressive arrogance in his reply. 'I never start trouble, mister — but I always finish it.'

With that, he nonchalantly swung one long leg clear of the stirrup and dismounted.

'Maybe he can help us?' Lucky spoke up. The tough old coot was well on the mend from his injury, and ready for revenge against the outlaws. 'Sheriff Dolby ain't due back fer another two days. We sure could use a manhunter on our side 'til he gets here with the US Marshal's men.'

'Lucky's got a point,' Eben agreed, looking at Corey and the others for their opinion.

'I ain't the law,' Lobart made his position clear.

'But yer on the side of the law,' Lucky reasoned.

Corey backed them up. 'If ya was willin' to help us out, we'd appreciate it. Copperstone is a peaceful town and we ain't used to dealin' with situations like this. Most of us fellers have women and children to fend for. The only one among us with any real deputy experience is Eben here.'

'An' I ain't as young as I used to be,' the old man retorted.

Lobart sighed, deep and heavy. 'What kinda trouble you folks in?'

'Outlaw trouble,' Eben informed him. 'They already killed our deputy and several others. We reckon they're on the run from the law, so there will be few towns safe for them to hideout in. They might come back to Copperstone thinkin' we're easy prey.'

'Them outlaws,' Lobart enquired, 'would they be the Catlin gang?'

'Don't know their names,' said Corey. 'But there were five altogether, one of them a Mexican.'

'Did the leader wear nothin' but black, includin' a black leather holster?' Lobart interjected.

'Yep,' Lucky confirmed. 'That's them.'

'Now they're in tow with a low-life varmint by the name of Jay,' Corey added.

'Jay who?'

Corey shrugged his shoulders. 'Nobody knows. Claimed he'd lost his memory. The doc's boy found him lyin' near the river. Everyone reckoned he struck his head and suffered amnesia. His personal belongings, gun, horse, money, everything were missin', makin' it seem like he'd been robbed and beaten.'

Lucky sighed with disappointment. 'Jay suckered all of us. We took him to be a decent sort.'

'Did he tell ya his name was Jay?' Lobart wanted to know, a hunch stirring in his gut.

'Nope,' replied Corey. 'Folks jest called him that 'cause of the tattoo on his arm. It was the letter J.'

149

'Jake!' Lobart suddenly realized who it was they were talking about.

'Ya know him?' Corey demanded.

'He's the friend I'm lookin' fer. Jake Farr.' He proceeded to confirm Jake's identity with a brief description. 'Got the tattoo on his upper arm. A tall, lean feller, aged about thirty. Favours a Smith and Wesson. Fights like a tiger.'

'Looks like your friend double-crossed ya,' Eben concluded. ' 'Cause he's ridin' with them outlaws yer after. An' one of'em is his brother.'

Lobart's brows drew together thoughtfully. 'Which one?'

'The one who wears black,' declared Lucky. 'When they was at the Mistral ranch, I heard him refer to Jay as his brother.'

'It jest don't make sense,' Lobart puzzled. 'Jake ain't got no brother, and he sure as hell wouldn't ride with the Catlin gang — least not by choice.'

'Nobody twisted his arm as far as we

could see,' Corey was adamant. 'That right boys?'

To a man, they all agreed.

'I was supposed to meet up with Jake a few days ago,' Lobart reflected aloud. 'It ain't like him to disappear without tellin' me where he was goin'. Jake's the most reliable man I ever met. Is it possible he really has lost his memory?'

By this time, Doc Lainey had joined the throng. 'In my professional opinion, he was definitely sufferin' from amnesia. He'd a bump the size of a man's fist on his head and a faraway look in his eyes as if everythin' was a mystery to him.'

'Then Jake might not know who he really is?' Lobart speculated.

'It's possible,' the doc confirmed. 'But we were suspicious of him 'cause he seemed to be on the side of them murderous outlaws.'

'I'll tell ya all somethin',' Lou-Lou's voice broke over the men's heads as she sauntered through the batwings of the

Sundown. 'That Catlin feller was lying. He told me straight he didn't have no brother.'

'What in tarnation are ya talkin' 'bout, woman?' Lucky queried, as he and the others turned their attention round to Lou-Lou.

'He said his name was Green,' she explained, 'but I didn't believe him. I reckoned he was a no-good sort an' he didn't want me knowin' who he was.'

'Did he mention about havin' a brother?' Corey asked.

'Nope, in fact it was me who brought the matter up. I thought Jay and him looked kinda like each other, ya know, the same tall, lean dark appearance and those stunnin' green eyes. Anyway, when I mentioned this to the feller in black, he denied havin' a brother.'

Lobart recalled something relevant. 'If I remember rightly, Lorn Catlin's only brother, Avery, was gunned down years ago in Arizona, along with their parents, when they were both kids.'

'Is it possible Lorn's lyin' to Jay,

sorry, Jake?' Lou-Lou corrected herself. 'Could he be pretendin' that Jake's his dead brother, Avery Catlin? Takin' advantage of Jake's loss of memory?'

'Lorn Catlin is a real devious character,' Lobart's heavy voice re-marked. 'He's capable of anythin'. On the surface, they could pass for brothers, so if Jake's lost his memory he might believe it's true.'

Everyone listening absorbed the possibility that Lorn had manipulated Jake Farr into believing he was his brother, and an outlaw.

'Who exactly is yer friend, Jake Farr?' Lou-Lou enquired of Lobart.

'Same as me,' he replied. 'A manhunter from Montana.'

'A manhunter!' Amber Lainey's voice trilled. Unable to keep her distance, and overhearing Jay's name mentioned, she'd edged her way over to listen to what the men and Lou-Lou were saying.

'Yes, ma'am. The best manhunter in the state of Montana. He's never failed to hunt down whoever he was after. We've been friends for four years, and I've never known him to let any criminals get away. Neither have I known him to do anything unlawful. He was always too darned honest.'

'Were both of ya huntin' the Catlin gang?' Amber asked, slightly breathless from everything she was discovering.

'Yep. Jake and I often team up when there's a gang to be hunted, especially when they're as bad as Lorn Catlin and his hard-killin' outlaws.'

Jake Farr? Amber spoke his name inwardly, listening to the sound of it inside her mind, trying it on for size and deciding it fitted just fine. Only Lou-Lou read the romantically hopeful expression in Amber's eyes. The two women exchanged a knowing glance, which happily by-passed the men in their company.

'Why don't ya come inside fer a drink, Kel Lobart?' Lou-Lou invited the manhunter.

'Reckon I'll do jest that, ma'am,'

he smiled, impressed by Lou-Lou's stunning femininity and her decisive manner.

All the townsmen present streamed into the Sundown. They had a heap of talking and planning to do, if they'd to help Lobart deal with the Catlin gang — and save Jake Farr from himself.

9

The Red Hot Poker saloon was aflame with gamblers and double-dealers. Gaudily dressed saloon girls draped themselves around those on whom fortune was smiling, while a jaded pianist jangled the keys of his tinny piano, barely audible above the rowdy revelry.

The large chandelier hanging from the ceiling was testimony that the Red Hot Poker had seen its fair share of gunfights, for there was hardly a piece of it intact. Stray bullets had shattered most of the crystal glass droplets, but somehow the savaged chandelier suited the violent ambience of this unruly establishment.

Jake Farr, believing he was Avery Catlin, sat at a round mahogany table in the centre of the saloon, along with Lorn and the gang. Together, they were awaiting the arrival of Owen Wexler.

Jake wore his new dark-green shirt tucked into the waistband of his jeans, with the Smith and Wesson holstered at his right hip. His thick sable hair was sleeked back from his harshly scupltured face and was still damp from his having recently dunked it in the wash basin upstairs in the room he was sharing with Lorn.

Both Lorn and Jake were washed but unshaven, the rough dark stubble on their strong chins giving them an even closer resemblance. Jake didn't know it, but unconsciously he was starting to look and act like a hard-living outlaw, unaware that the Catlin gang were his sworn enemies.

Glancing at him, Lorn couldn't help but wonder when Jake was going to remember the truth. However, since their arrival in Redville, he'd seen no outward sign that Jake was returning to his old self. In fact, Jake seemed to be taking to the role of his brother quite naturally. This bothered Lorn, because he was beginning to take a liking to Jake. Even though they hailed from opposite sides of the law, as men there was an easy communication and understanding between them. Although Lorn had known Silvano and the others for some time, the brotherly rapport he was developing with the manhunter, was different. There was a time when he'd have relished killing Jake, but things had changed, and he wasn't looking forward to the day when he might have to put a bullet in him. Jake was the brother he never had, but often wanted. If Avery and his parents hadn't been murdered, Lorn believed his life might not have gone so wrong. Instead, fate had dealt him a dark hand, and he was playing it in the only way he knew how.

'Somethin' botherin' ya, Roscoe?' Sparks asked, knowing something was always worrying Roscoe. It was just a matter of getting him to spit it out before it got stuck in his throat and choked him.

Roscoe's slat-thin frame was sitting as if on hot coals, edgily stroking his thin stringy moustache. He accepted that he was a born worrier, but tonight, he felt his apprehension was justified.

'What in heck's name's gnawin' at ya?' Lorn snapped. The last thing he needed was a nervous jack-rabbit sitting beside him when Wexler was due to arrive any minute.

'D'ya think another posse from Copperstone will come after us here in Redville?' Roscoe sounded jittery. 'Their sheriff might have returned by now with reinforcements. An' surely they'll figger this is where we'd head for.' He paused, then added, 'D'ya suppose they'll come an' git us?'

Lorn answered calmly. 'Nope, they won't want to come to this rough hell-hole. Probably, they'll jest wire the Redville sheriff's office an' tell 'em to be on the lookout for any suspicious characters.' Lorn then laughed smugly. 'An' this town is full to burstin' with 'em.'

Roscoe smiled and relaxed. He trusted Lorn's judgement. It had never let him down yet.

'Here comes Wexler now,' Sparks suddenly whispered.

'Let me do most of the talkin',' Lorn advised them. 'An' remember, this banker is money in our pockets, so don't go gittin' him riled up.' This particular warning was directed specifically at Silvano.

'I don't like him,' Silvano hissed, 'but I won't say nothin' to upset the fat, greedy, smart-mouthed cuss.'

Kid Yerby sniggered.

Lorn threw them both a silencing glare.

Fat, fifty, wearing a city-style suit and derby hat, Owen Wexler looked like a banker. Wexler's waistcoat was stretched taut across his flabby paunch, as was the chain of his gold pocket watch. The air in the saloon was hot and smoky, causing Wexler's red-veined face to sweat profusely. This of course wasn't the only reason he was sweating. Dealing with the Catlin gang was a risky business.

'Howdy, boys,' Wexler gasped, as if trying to suck in from the thick atmosphere all the oxygen his obese body craved.

'Sit down,' Lorn invited him to join them.

Wexler squeezed himself in between Lorn and Silvano. 'Everyone expects me to hustle newcomers to deposit their money in my bank, so no one will think there's anything untoward goin' on between us,' the banker explained. 'In fact, if I didn't hustle ya, then they'd be suspicious.' This was Wexler's joke, though it was quite true.

'Don't think I remember you, feller,' said Wexler, observing Jake through beady eyes overhung with fatty folds of skin.

'This here's my brother, Avery,' Lorn was quick to dispel the banker's wariness. 'Ya didn't git to meet him last time we was in town, 'cause Avery was busy keepin' the saloon girls company,' he winked.

Jake was astonished at being tagged a womanizer. Immediately, his mind sifted through his feelings for Amber Lainey, then his appreciation of Lou-Lou. He had to admit that he found both of them real huggable and kissable. Was this, he pondered, the womanizer in him stirring?

'Got a tattoo on his arm,' Lorn continued, latching on to this prime opportunity to explain away the initial J. Earlier, when they'd been getting washed and changed, Jake had queried why he had the tattoo and what it stood for. Stuck for a straight and plausible answer, Lorn pretended not to hear. Now a reason had come to him, wicked though it was. 'It's a letter J,' Lorn grinned. 'Know what it stands for?'

Nobody at the table had a clue. The outlaws were silently expectant, wondering what contrived lie Lorn had up his sleeve.

'It stands for Jezebel,' Lorn laughed. 'Avery sure is one for the ladies.'

Wexler was content with Lorn's stream of lies. 'I kinda like the Jezebel sort myself,' he leered. 'Got plenty of life in 'em, an' ya don't have to live with 'em afterwards either.'

Everyone agreed with this particular sentiment, except Jake. He was too deep in his own thoughts. Casting his mind back to Verity Garrett, he recalled her mentioning that his J tattoo might not represent his own name — and she was right. A heavy sigh escaped his unsmiling mouth. He'd never have guessed he was a womanizing outlaw with a passion for Jezebels. What other deep, dark character traits were lurking in his background? He shuddered to imagine.

'Wanna drink?' Sparks asked Wexler, sliding over a bottle of red-eye and a used glass.

'Never drink when I'm doin' business,' Wexler puffed.

'Then let's git right down to it,' Lorn

enthused. 'Does our original deal still stand?'

'Indeed it does, Lorn. Nothin's changed at the bank and the railroad wages will arrive as usual tomorrow around noon,' he shrugged heavily. 'Ya could do the job tomorrow night, unless ya want to wait until the next delivery which would give ya more time to plan the details.'

'The details are fixed firm inside my head,' Lorn announced. 'We'll do the job tomorrow night. The sooner we git it done and outa Redville the better.'

'Good. I was hopin' ya'd say that,' Wexler's fleshy mouth smiled. 'Because on top of the railroad money, there's a pile of cash sittin' in the bank right now. We've had a heap of big gamblers in town.'

'We'll arrive at the bank just before closing time,' Lorn underlined the details for Wexler's benefit. 'Invite us into your office and we'll hide there until after ya lock-up. Once we've got the money, we'll tie ya up and leave without bein' seen through the back entrance.'

'An' ya know exactly where my house is?' Wexler emphasized.

'Don't worry, we'll leave your share under your front porch.' Lorn smiled. His fairness was tangible, but his power to kill was equally strong.

A cold sweat drained across Wexler's bloated face, hoping he'd made the right decision to trust the outlaws. Either way, it was too late now to back out, if he wanted to survive.

At the next table, a rabble of four rough characters began amusing themselves by shattering whiskey glasses with a whip.

The tip of the long leather whip accidently sliced across the back of Lorn's neck, causing him to wince. The whip's forked-tie was weighted with lead shot, and although it hadn't torn open Lorn's skin, it had left a bright red welt where it had hit him.

Jake was the first to retaliate, throwing back his chair as he got to his feet. 'Be more careful where yer crackin' that darn whip,' Jake's deep-timbre voice shouted at the offenders.

The holder of the whip was the human equivalent of a rattle-snake — a long, thin, slippery cuss with a rasping voice. His face was as rough as the leather boots on his feet — and both had seen better days. He gave Jake a bone-jarring stare. 'Ya talkin' to me?'

'Ain't nobody else in here using a whip,' Jake remarked bluntly.

'Ya gonna let him talk to ya like that, Griff?' one of Griff's three sidewinders enflamed the situation.

Griff spat a mouthful of well-chewed tobacco directly at Jake, missing him by a whisker. 'Ya got two choices, feller: crawl outa here right now like a dog on yer hands and knees grateful I didn't kill ya, or stay, and end up bein' carried out by yer yellow-livered friend.' Griff intentionally referred to Lorn.

Lorn went to retaliate, but Jake barred his way with a restraining arm. 'That's my brother, an' when ya mess with him, ya mess with me,' Jake snarled.

This was fighting talk.

Eager to use his whip on something more challenging than empty glasses, Griff lashed out with the whip, snaking it venomously towards Jake's face.

With lightning reflexes, Jake snatched the whip's tip with his bare hands as it hissed through the air, tearing it clean out of Griff's astounded grasp.

Skilfully, Jake reeled-in the pleated leather handle, catching it with his right hand and wielding it expertly.

Sensing the drama in their midst, those nearby moved away a safe distance. Like dropping a pebble into a pool of water, everyone in the centre of the saloon rippled quickly to the outer edges. Here, they were able to see the fight without getting sliced to ribbons in the process.

Wexler joined the outer limits, while the Catlin gang, well aware of Jake Farr's prowess with a whip, simply eased themselves back a ways to give the manhunter more room to manoeuvre.

'If ya leave now, I'll say no more about this incident,' Jake stated in his authoritative voice, giving Griff and his men the chance to leave quietly.

They didn't want to leave quietly. In fact, they were itching for trouble. Unluckily for them, Jake had the ideal weapons with which to scratch it for them.

Griff stared at Jake with undiluted viciousness, his fingers twitching near the Walker-Colt slung at his hip.

Giving the whip an uncoiling shake, Jake prepared to take action against whatever Griff had in mind.

A split second later, Griff clawed the revolver from its holster with the intention of killing Jake, but the manhunter asserted the whip with greater speed, cracking the Walker-Colt out of Griff's gun-hand before he could pull the trigger. Then, in a blistering second, Jake sliced the whip across Griff's chest. It cut through his shirt and drew blood, a gash running from one shoulder diagonally downwards to his rib cage.

'Anyone else figgerin' on goin' fer their gun?' Jake was defiant.

There were no takers.

Griff's three sidewinders had considered for a second whether to retaliate, their fingers loitering near their holstered revolvers. However, they thought better of it.

Griff was moaning from the searing pain of his wound.

'Take yer friend an' git outa here,' Jake commanded. 'An' don't let me see your faces again while I'm in town.'

Retreating under the intense rage in Jake's eyes, the frustrated gunslingers gathered up Griff and helped him to the door of the saloon.

Everyone cleared the way for them to leave.

'I'll git even with ya for this, I swear I will,' Griff rasped, regaining some of his wounded composure as he leaned on the batwings for support.

'If ya ever threaten me again, I'll hunt ya down and kill ya fer sure,' Jake retorted, his voice deep and darkly powerful. 'There ain't no man livin' I cain't hunt down if I put my mind to it, so ya better steer well clear of me.'

Unknowingly, Jake was reverting to his manhunting ways. Realizing this, the Catlin gang froze in tense silence, their eyes questioning each other. Had Jake suddenly got his memory back?

'Ya OK, Brother?' Jake turned to Lorn, effectively dispelling their concern.

'Yep. I'm jest fine, Avery,' Lorn nodded, breathing a private sigh of relief that Jake was still none the wiser as to his real identity.

As Griff and his men exited, the saloon slowly returned to its normal state of bawdy revelry.

Wexler came back over to the Catlin outlaws. 'I can see I'm dealin' with true professionals,' he complimented them, pleased to be on their side. 'Never knew anyone who was faster with a

whip than a feller could draw his gun,'
he acknowledged to Jake.

Lorn interjected confidently, 'An'
Avery's faster with his Smith and
Wesson than he is with a whip.'

10

Noon, the following day, Jake and Kid Yerby were unobtrusively watching for the arrival of the railroad wages from their vantage point inside Redville's barber's shop. Situated adjacent to the bank, they had a prime view from the barber's shop window as they sat side by side awaiting a shave.

It was a firm rule that all customers must hang their holstered guns up on the hooks which were provided on entering the barber's establishment. Jake and Kid Yarby had to abide by that rule, and were sitting unarmed in their respective swivel chairs with white coverings draped around their persons and small towels wrapped around their necks.

Stropping the ivory-handled open razor, the barber lathered the soap liberally on to Jake's heavily stubbled chin and began to shave with skilful speed and accuracy. Tactfully, no idle chatter was entered into, the barber having learned the hard way that asking an intrusive question to the wrong man could get him into big trouble.

Being the only other customer, Kid Yerby waited his turn, his deceivingly innocent blue eyes vigilantly watching the bank opposite.

It was part of Lorn's plan that two of the gang would ensure the railroad money arrived as Wexler had promised. Jake said he'd gladly go to the barber's. He was keen to see that Wexler wasn't lying, and get himself a clean shave into the bargain. Kid Yerby agreed to accompany him, though the blond downy wisps which grew on his boyish chin hardly qualified for the attention of a barber's razor. Jake reckoned the Kid simply wanted to prove his maturity with such a visit, though he also reckoned the Kid had reached a killer's maturity which most law-abiding men would never realize.

At least, not if they were lucky.

Two minutes past noon, the stagecoach drew up in front of the bank to deposit the railroad wages.

Kid Yarby turned his head to smile at Jake, their eyes silently acknowledging Wexler had told the truth.

However, there was something about the way Kid Yerby smiled at Jake that bothered him; it was an untrue smile, and the way he laughed, a sort of immature chortle with a hint of secret cruelty. Inside and out, the Kid was two different young men. An angelic, wholesome façade hid the sadistic monster of his true self.

A cold shiver spidered its way along Jake's spine. Something lurking deep his mind warned him that he was trapped in a web of lies and deceit. The warning was loud, but unclear. He tried to force himself to remember. Underneath the voluminous white covering, his hands gripped tight to the arms of the barber's chair. He had to remember, he chided himself.

It was important!

'Almost done,' the barber reassured him, mistaking Jake's tension for a fear of the razor slipping. Deftly, the barber finished up by placing a soothing damp towel over Jake's face, persuading him to relax back in the chair for a couple of minutes while the towel calmed his newly shaven skin.

Having seen the railroad wages arrive safely, Jake lay there with his eyes closed and face covered while the barber shaved Kid Yerby.

It was a mistake Jake Farr would never repeat again. While his eyes were shut and the Kid's head was tilted back looking at the ceiling, Griff and his three sidewinders stealthily entered the barber's shop. Griff was mentally still stinging from his whipping.

Griff silently motioned with the barrel of his Walker-Colt for the barber to leave quickly and quietly. He didn't need telling twice and made himself as scarce as snow in the desert.

Several seconds passed before the

Kid noticed nobody was shaving him. When he looked round, his startled blue eyes stared straight into the barrel of Griff's revolver. The seething snarl on Griff's thin, bloodless lips warned the Kid not to move a muscle.

Powerless without his guns, which were still hanging up on the wall, the Kid reluctantly obeyed the voiceless warning. Inwardly, he was pinning his hopes on Jake being able to deal with the situation. If ever Jake needed every fighting skill he possessed — it was now!

'I warned ya I'd git even,' Griff growled through yellow, gritted teeth, poking his gun into Jake's ribs.

With his face still masked by the damp towel, Jake remained uncannily calm.

This disturbed Griff and his men. No man they'd ever come across would sit there, calm as a midnight lake.

The Kid was mentally crossing his fingers that Jake hadn't fallen asleep and was aware of the danger they were in.

Griff gave Jake's ribs another poke with his gun, this time harder, urging him to react, to panic. He wanted to smell the fear on Jake's worthless body before he killed him. He wanted to taste his terror.

Jake didn't budge.

Unable to stand it any more, Griff swiped the towel from Jake's face.

This action was the equivalent of opening a tiger's cage.

With almost inhuman speed, Jake let rip with a debilitating punch to Griff's spindle-boned face, cracking his jaw into dislocation. Griff dropped like a ton of lead.

Horrified, Griff's three sidewinders hesitated for the split second Jake needed to throw the white covering he was wearing over the nearest attacker and fell him unconscious with the barber's chair. The remaining duo fired two shots at Jake, but he lifted the barber's dense metal tray up as a shield, causing the bullets to ricochet wildly, shattering a large mirror into smithereens.

Both attacking gunmen dived to the floor for cover as stray bullets and shards of mirror sprayed about them. Kid Yerby was knocked backwards, his chair toppled over and his head struck the unyielding floor stunning him out of action.

In the mêlée, Jake kicked the sidewinders' guns out of their unco-ordinated and flustered grips. Both revolvers slid across the floor to a far corner of the shop, well out of their grasp.

Without guns, the two faced up to Jake, both of them grabbing hold of the barber's open razors which were lying on a nearby shelf. Pace by pace, they closed in on Jake, their hatchet faces willing and ready to rip him apart.

Jake instinctively knew he'd never had a razor fight before, but he steeled himself to make this the first victory.

Beside him was the barber's large,

ivory-handled, cut-throat razor. A deadly weapon in the wrong hands. Jake picked it up, figuring this evened the score.

Both men attacked him at once, slashing randomly with the razors. Jake sustained several nicks, mainly on his hands, as he defended himself.

Fearlessly, Jake countered their attack, slicing across one of their arms. Blood spurted from the wound, causing the man to back off warily. The other man flashed the razor at Jake's throat like a man possessed. Jake weaved back and forth out of harm's way, eventually slashing him in retaliation along the gut. He collapsed, landing on Griff's prone body.

Seeing this, the last remaining sidewinder turned and, clutching the gash on his arm, scarpered, leaving Jake standing amid the heavy silence which reeked with the stench of blood, sweat and stale fear.

'Ya awright?' Jake helped Kid Yerby to his feet. A mite unsteady, he was, nevertheless, astounded by Jake's prowess. 'Let's git ya back to the Red Hot Poker,' the manhunter urged him, offering a strong arm as support to head the Kid out.

There was no repercussion from the sheriff's office. That was the way of things in Redville, especially as nobody had actually died. Broken bones and spilled guts didn't take priority. Violence was so frequent, so ingrained into everyday life, that all it took was a few buckets of water to wash away the blood — and the barber's shop was open for business as usual.

* * *

Lorn checked his watch. 'Almost time to go, boys. Everyone ready?'

The Catlin gang were ready.

'Then let's go do it,' Lorn gave the command, setting the wheels of the bank robery in motion.

Roscoe and Sparks were to position themselves at the rear of the bank to cover their getaway. Jake, Lorn, Silvano and Kid Yerby were to mosey casually into the bank, allowing Wexler to usher them into his private office.

The early evening air was warm and mellow, the town's main street bathed in a golden glow of the forthcoming sunset.

'The bank's about to close in the next five minutes,' an unsuspecting bank clerk briskly informed the foursome as they entered the building.

Lorn pasted a strangely unnerving smile on his cold features. 'Our business won't take long.' It was a smile which could manipulate the innocent into doing exactly what he wanted. Right now, he wanted the naive young man with his hornrimmed spectacles and pathetic brown suit to mind his own business. The clerk did just that, finding someone else to pursue with his clock-watching.

'Can I help you gentlemen?' Wexler came puffing towards them.

'We're considering makin' a very

large withdrawal,' Lorn jested in a low voice.

Wexler grinned. 'Then ya came to the right place. Come into my private office and we'll discuss how I can help ya.'

The foursome stayed there out of sight until Wexler told them the coast was clear, after he'd secured the bank for the evening when everyone had gone.

'The safe's over here,' said Wexler, sweating, leading them to it, his hands fumbling through a bundle of keys searching for the one which opened the safe.

From under their coats and jackets, the foursome produced several canvas sacks which they intended stuffing brim-full with dollars.

'Help yourselves, boys,' Wexler spread his arms wide in a generous gesture, having unlocked the safe to reveal its fortune.

Silvano and Kid Yerby filled the sacks, while Lorn tied them tight to prevent the money escaping.

Jake somehow couldn't bring himself to touch one single dollar. Something was wrong. Terribly wrong. He found it hard to imagine that he'd robbed numerous banks before. Maybe losing his memory was the best thing that had ever happened to him, he mused, standing back and watching his brother grab fistfuls of dollars. Maybe the amnesia had caused him to lose his taste for stealing? Whatever was bothering him, he was glad this was to be their final robbery. 'I'll go check the back entrance,' Jake excused himself.

'Here's the key, Avery,' said Wexler, handing it to him. 'I'll go git the ropes so ya can tie me to my chair.' The banker scuttled off to his office to fetch the ropes, anxious to ensure they'd remember to hog-tie him before they made their getaway.

Jake took the key and headed for the back entrance. He was scowling as he walked, trying to sort out his turbulent emotions.

A hail of gunfire erupting from outside shocked him out of his rancour. He swithered whether or not to open the rear door in case the law had gotten wind of the robbery and were trying to smoke them out into the open. So, instead, he peered through a small, heavily-barred window. Lorn was at Jake's side within seconds. 'What's happenin', Avery?'

The scene from the window was self-explanatory. In a blinding flash of bullets, Griff and his men, although worse for wear from their last encounter with Jake, had gunned down Sparks and Roscoe. There was nothing Jake or Lorn could do. The hail of bullets had killed them for sure.

'Hell's fire,' Lorn swore. Jake wondered if it was for the loss of his friends, or the disruption of the robbery? Either way, they were all in big trouble.

Silvano and the Kid came hurrying as best they could, loaded down with the money-bags.

'Wexler's tied-up,' Silvano hissed. 'What's all the gunfire?'

Lorn's voice was void of any emotion. 'Griff and his man jest killed Sparks and Roscoe,' he stated quickly, wasting no time.

Outside, Griff and his gang hurriedly rummaged through Sparks' and Roscoe's pockets for anything worth stealing, unaware the rest of the Catlin gang were inside the bank.

Lorn turned in deadly seriousness to Kid Yerby. 'Kid?' he beckoned with a curt movement of his head.

The Kid knew what he meant.

'Unlock the door, Avery,' Lorn requested, sweeping his long black coat away from the guns on either side of his lean hips. Kid Yerby did likewise with his buckskin jacket. Both men were ready for action.

Without hesitation Jake turned the key and clicked the door open.

Lorn and the Kid stepped outside. The Griff gang were still busy with their murdered prey and didn't see them coming.

By the time they realized, they were looking death in the face.

Lorn and Kid Yerby's revolvers cleared leather with outstanding speed, firing with a force, accuracy and velocity unmatchable by the Griff gang. Their targets died in seconds in a hail of lead.

Holstering their smoking revolvers, Lorn and the Kid urged Jake and Silvano to make haste. Jake hurriedly locked the rear door of the bank so no one would suspect it had been robbed. Quickly, the foursome then divided the money-bags, and made a run for their horses which were tethered out back. Luckily for them, another gun-fight had broken out in the main street over gambling debts and this drew the sheriff's and his deputies' attention away for the vital minutes it took for the Catlin outlaws to make their escape.

On the outskirts of Redville, they

halted to discuss what they were going to do. Originally, the plan was for Sparks and Roscoe to stash Wexler's money under his porch. This task was now allocated to Lorn and Jake.

'We'll deliver Wexler's money, then catch up with ya later. Wexler's house is on the outskirts of town, so there's little danger of us bein' caught.'

'D'ya want the Kid and me to head for the hills as planned?' asked Silvano.

'Yep. Nothin' else changes.'

As far as Silvano was concerned, plenty had changed. His jet-black eyes targeted straight at Jake. There was no mistaking their message. The Mexican blamed Jake for the death of Sparks and Roscoe.

'If ya got somethin' to say to me,' Jake snapped at the Mexican, 'spit it out now.'

'We'll settle this later,' Lorn stated firmly. 'Let's git goin' before the law's on our tails.'

'We'll settle this now!' Silvano's rage was making him foolhardy. 'It's 'cause of you that Roscoe and Sparks are dead,' he hissed venomously at Jake.

The tension in the air between Jake and the Mexican was tangible, both men grimly intent on settling their differences with a fight.

'What's it to be Silvano?' Jake's deep voice rumbled.

Silvano pulled a large, serrated hunting knife out of his saddle and leaped down from his horse. 'No guns, jest you and me.'

As Jake dismounted to take up the challenge, Lorn shouted, 'There'll be no killin'. We need each other right now if we're all to survive.'

'Don't worry Lorn, I ain't gonna kill . . . ' Silvano hesitated, almost making the mistake of calling him Jake, 'I won't kill *Avery*,' he corrected his near error.

'First blood drawn, then it's over,' Lorn announced the rules, fully believing Jake could handle Silvano without either of them getting badly hurt.

'Agreed,' Silvano muttered under his

breath, lunging at Jake with the blade in a determined attempt to catch him off-guard and slice the first blood.

With both hands fisted and wrists firmly together to form his arms into the shape of a cross, Jake deftly blocked the attack, catching hold of Silvano's wrist in the process and disarming him of the knife, which he threw straight-bladed into the ground.

Silvano gave himself a shake. He knew Jake was good, but he never thought the manhunter could disarm him so swiftly. Neither did he imagine Jake would then proceed to rain a torrent of blows at his body and face, drawing blood from his nose.

'First blood,' Jake asserted.

Before Silvano could even think of retaliating, Lorn called a halt. 'It's over! Now, let's git goin'.'

Silvano wasn't satisfied. Pulling his hunting knife out of the ground he sheathed it back in his saddle. Then, mounting his pinto so he could look down on Jake, he menaced in a voice throbbing with hate, 'Another time, another place.'

Looking up at Silvano, Jake lost no power of stature whatsoever. 'Any time, any place.' His tone was as dark as the crack of doom.

As the two pairs rode off on their separate ways, Silvano was beginning to regret ever crossing Jake Farr. The manhunter was sure living up to his reputation as a mean, tough-fighting cuss who would track his prey down to the bitter end.

* * *

The deep, quiet stillness that only comes at night surrounded Jake and Lorn as they rode towards Wexler's house on the edge of Redville.

Conversation had been dry, but the silence comfortable, neither man feeling the urge to talk much.

Jake certainly preferred the company of his own mixed-up thoughts. Flashes of memory were coming back to him in disjointed pieces which refused to stick together, causing him confusion.

Now and then he wondered what thoughts were running through Lorn's mind, but something held him back from asking. He had the strangest hunch that the answers, if true, wouldn't be to his liking.

Foremost in Jake's flashes was the smile on Kid Yerby's face when they were in the barber's shop, and later, the killer expression on his boyish features as he prepared to gun down the Griff gang. Then, there was the dark figure of Lorn, sweeping back his long black coat to reveal the revolvers he could wield with exceptional speed. And the silver skeleton charm worn by Silvano also troubled him deeply.

Everything felt wrong. The bank robbery, the cold-blooded killings, everything. Nothing made a darn bit of sense, especially as he felt no regret or angst about fighting fellers with either his bare fists, a whip or a cut-throat razor. The latter incidents were certainly made in self-defence, almost as if he was lawfully righting wrongs.

'That's Wexler's place jest ahead.' Lorn pointed to a fair-sized, redwood house. 'Looks like Wexler ain't home yet.'

'What about his family? How d'ya know they ain't at home?'

A wry grin stretched across Lorn's mouth. 'Wexler's too greedy to share his life with anyone. He lives alone.'

Wasting no more time, Lorn rode over, leaned down from his horse and threw the sack of money into the hiding place under the porch.

'Reckon the law don't know Wexler's tied up inside the bank,' Lorn concluded. 'Anyways, it's best no one discovers him until the morning. It'll be more believable.'

'Will he be awright until tomorrow morning?' Jake questioned.

Lorn sneered sardonically. 'That fat bloodsucker would survive for a week if he thought he'd git a sack of money at the end of it.'

11

Dark pine-shadowed hills were outlined against the night sky. Silvano and Kid Yerby ascended the rolling peaks, arriving on a sage-covered plateau overlooking the vastness of the northern Californian plain. Two hours' ride from Redville, the hilltop hideaway was where they planned to rest and await Jake and Lorn.

With the horses unsaddled and the outlaws' share of the money-bags safely by their side, they kindled a small camp-fire and ate beef jerky washed down with coffee.

'Thought I heard somethin',' Silvano suddenly started, his jet eyes searching the surrounding darkness which was illuminated only by the fire's glow.

'I don't hear nothin',' the Kid assured him, chewing on his jerky. 'Yer jest jittery 'cause the plan's been changed.'

Silvano's eyes trailed over the obscure blackness once more before he settled back and relaxed.

'Think Lorn's turned soft?' Silvano asked.

Kid Yerby raised a shrewd, blond eyebrow. 'I think he'd like it if Jake really was his brother. Come to think of it, I wouldn't mind havin' him in our gang. He's mighty useful. Certainly wouldn't want him as an enemy agin'.'

'There's gonna come a time when Jake remembers everythin',' Silvano warned ominously.

The Kid nodded. 'Hopefully we'll be long gone over the border to Mexico by then.'

'If he don't hurry up and remember who he is, maybe he'll want to come with us to Mexico?'

'Hell's teeth. Wouldn't that be galdarned typical,' the Kid sighed.

'One of us would have to kill him if that happened,' Silvano underlined.

'Reckon yer faster than he is?'

Silvano hesitated. This was answer enough.

A faint rustling sound emanating from the blackness curtailed the outlaws' conversation.

Their faces, lit by the flames of the fire, froze. Only their eyes, wide and wary, remained alive in their still features.

'Don't move a muscle, fellers,' a sombre voice echoed out of nowhere.

Despite the warning, both outlaws instinctively jumped to their feet and reached for their revolvers.

The shadowed interloper immediately pumped a full load from his rifle into the camp-fire, causing sparks to erupt around their boots like shooting stars in a midnight velvet sky.

'That's your second warning,' the unseen voice shouted menacingly. 'There won't be a third!'

The outlaws held their guns in check, hearing the stranger instantly reload his rifle.

'What d'ya want?' Kid Yerby called

out in a reedy tone.

'I want ya to drop your guns. I'm taking ya back to Montana where ya'll be tried for the crimes ya committed there.'

'That you Jake?' Silvano murmured tentatively. The deepness of the voice and the Montana accent was similar to Jake's, but the Mexican was unsure if it was him. In a flash, it crossed his mind that Jake might have got his memory back, killed Lorn, and was now set on capturing them.

In answer to Silvano's question, Kel Lobart stepped out from the shadows, armed with his rifle which was targeted on the outlaws. The long silver hair beneath his grey stetson glinted in the firelight, as did his keen steel-grey eyes.

'Lobart,' Kid Yarby gasped. The manhunter was the last person he expected to see.

'I'm takin' ya both in,' Lobart stated with a force which denied them any other option.

'Cain't let ya do that,' Silvano rasped.

No sooner had the words escaped the Mexican's determined lips, than Kid Yerby opened fire on the manhunter, estimating he was fast enough to kill him. He estimated wrong. A split second too slow to beat the rifle, the Kid got his heart blown clean out.

Silvano dived behind a rock for cover, his silver-handled Colts stinging the night air with bullets, none of which hit Lobart, who himself had dropped to the ground and rolled over towards some low-lying boulders.

Under cover of darkness, Silvano swiftly made his escape into the thickness of the nearby pine trees.

Lobart went after him.

Stalking his prey, the manhunter ventured further into the trees, listening for any sound to guide him to the right direction. Hearing nothing, he reckoned the Mexican was hiding, waiting to gun him down. There was only one way to beat him, Lobart concluded — the hunter's way. He'd lie in wait 'till Silvano was forced to make the first move. And when he did, he'd have him dead to rights. Without his horse, Silvano was going nowhere.

Not realizing the manhunter's ploy, Silvano eventually fell straight into Lobart's trap. Although he attempted to move with the utmost silence, the lucky charm on the sleeve of his jacket led Lobart right to him. In the darkness, the sound of the silver skeleton's bones rattling echoed in the stillness.

Lobart closed his eyes, letting his inner senses guide his rifle. Feeling he was dead on target, he squeezed the trigger, and sent the message of death into Silvano's chest. Lobart knew his bullet had struck the outlaw by the muffled cry which rang out in the moonless night.

Keeping his rifle alert, Lobart carefully picked his way towards Silvano, who was lying gasping his last. Seeing the Mexican was no longer a threat, Lobart quickly kneeled down beside him. 'Where's Jake Farr?' he demanded deeply.

Silvano gave a gurgled laugh as the blood oozed from his mouth, staining his teeth bright crimson. 'On his way to Hell, I hope!'

'Tell me where he is, dammit! Do one last decent thing before ya die.'

'Go rot in Hell, Lobart. You're just as bad as me. Ya kill for money too.' Giving one last tortured grin, he coughed another mouthful of blood, and died.

★ ★ ★

Lobart dumped the bodies of Kid Yarby and Silvano in Redville. He received written proof from the sheriff that he'd successfully hunted down two members of the Catlin gang. Lobart also handed over the money-bags once he realized they belonged to the town's bank. Although it was barely half of the amount that was stolen, the sheriff was mighty grateful. For all his efforts,

Lobart would gain substantial rewards.

Now uppermost in his mind was to find Jake. Unless he'd gotten his memory back, he feared his friend was living on borrowed time in the company of Lorn Catlin.

★ ★ ★

Two days later, Jake and Lorn had given up searching the area for Silvano and Kid Yerby.

In the tree-shaded bend of a river which snaked between Redville and Copperstone, they paused to rest and water the horses. The noon-day sun was splitting through the cobalt blue sky, reflecting off the meandering river.

'They're either dead, or they've scarpered with their share of the money,' Lorn concluded as they filled their flasks with cool, refreshing water. 'Either way, we cain't spend any more time scouting around for them. This area ain't safe. We've got more than enough money for ourselves. It's time we headed for Mexico.'

'We'll need some fresh supplies for the journey,' Jake spluttered, splashing handfuls of water over his sweat-beaded face. 'Where's the nearest town that's safe for us to buy what we need?'

'There's a place just south of Copperstone where nobody really knows us. We'll load up there, then continue heading south.' He glanced up at the vibrant sky. 'It's too hot to travel this time of day. We'll rest here until late afternoon, then be on our way.'

Jake swept his soaking wet hair back from his strong, lean face. 'In the meantime, I could go hunt us somethin' to eat?'

Lorn didn't doubt it, but he wanted to keep Jake within his sight. 'Tell ya what,' he suggested, as an alternative, 'why don't ya catch us some fish from the river? Ya was always good at that when we was kids.'

'Suits me, Brother,' Jake agreed, stripping off his shirt and boots.

Wading across halfway until he was

waist-deep in water, Jake then stood perfectly still, his hands cupped ready to scoop up any passing fish and throw them on to the riverbank.

Lorn sat under the shade of a low-hanging tree, watching Jake, occasionally casting him a nod and smile of encouragement.

The glint of a rifle poking through the greenery on the opposite side of the river suddenly caught Lorn's eyes. As far as he could determine, it was a solitary figure, not a posse, but it was a threat none the less.

'Avery,' Lorn hissed in a whispered voice, catching Jake's attention.

Wondering what was wrong, Jake squinted at him against the glare of the sun.

Jake could see by the urgent expression on Lorn's face that something was troubling him. It was then Jake had the strangest feeling someone was watching him from the other side of the river. With his back towards whoever it was, he could only guess at their presence.

Stepping out into the open, Kel Lobart, brandishing his rifle, shouted loudly, 'Jake!'

At the sound of his name, Jake turned round in the water to find his friend, Kel Lobart waving at him. In the moment as he spun around, his memory whirred back into place as if it had never been away. His whole life was back to normal.

'Kel,' he smiled broadly, relieved and excited that his memory had returned. Standing there, in the middle of the river, he remembered everything.

He recalled in detail, a year ago when he started hunting the Catlin gang in Montana with the help of Kel Lobart, how Silvano had shot him in the chest. Luckily the bullet had struck his gold pocket watch which saved his life. Thrown back by the force of the bullet, Jake hadn't been able to retaliate and the Mexican had escaped.

Silvano also tried to kill him again, this time at the Copperstone river. Kid Yarby and the Mexican had bushwhacked him, intent of giving him a slow, torturous death. Jake had gotten too close to the Catlin gang trail, knowing they were heading north to rob the bank in Redville. Lorn and the others had ridden hard, leaving Silvano and the Kid to finish Jake off. The last thing Jake remembered was falling from his startled horse on to the rocky ground. Clearly, the outlaws must have assumed he'd struck his head and died. They'd stripped his body of all identity, so nobody, especially his partner, Kel Lobart, would realize what had happened. Once the vultures had done their worst, they figured he would be unrecognizable. Fortunately for Jake, young Derry Lainey found him and got him to the doc in time.

His nightmares about the silver skeleton shooting him in the chest now made sense. And so too did Lorn's trap of calling him Avery.

Burning with rage, Jake glared daggers at Lorn, the distance between them no barrier for the ferocity of his anger.

Lorn knew Jake Farr was back with a vengeance!

Grabbing hold of his horse's reins, Lorn leaped into the saddle, making a quick getaway with his share of the money. The bullets from Lobart's rifle whizzed passed him as he rode off like wildfire.

* * *

The two manhunters caught up with each other's news as they made a brief stop at Redville. The sheriff was content with their explanation of Jake's innocent involvement in the bank robbery, especially when he handed over a money-bag full of dollars. Only two sacks of stolen money remained to be accounted for. Jake said Lorn had one sack and Wexler had the other, telling the sheriff all about Wexler's cheating ways. He also mentioned about the shoot-out at the rear of the bank. However, Jake soon realized the sheriff didn't give a hoot who killed

Griff and his sidewinders — it was one less troublesome gang for him to worry about.

With all loose ends tied up in Redville, Jake and Lobart then headed for Copperstone where other matters needed attending to before they decided what to do about Lorn Catlin.

Amber was delighted to see Jake Farr. 'Come in, Jake.' She welcomed him into her father's house, savouring the taste of his real name. The welcome from Doc Lainey and Derry was equally warm, but sensing Amber and Jake wanted to be alone, the doc and his young son gave them peace and privacy to do their romancing.

'I never thought I'd see ya again,' Amber beamed, hardly able to take her wide topaz eyes from his face.

'I never thought I'd be back,' Jake told her honestly. 'Thought I'd burned too many bridges in my wake.'

'But everythin's settled now, ain't it?' she wanted assurance. 'Sheriff Dolby and the US Marshals have confirmed that you're a free man?'

'Yep,' Jake said with relief. 'An' I have Kel Lobart to thank for helpin' me.'

'He's a good and trusted friend,' Amber confirmed. 'Where is he?'

Jake grinned sheepishly. 'Makin' eyes at Lou-Lou.'

Amber giggled. 'She sure likes Kel. I think they make quite a well-matched couple.'

Jake pulled Amber into his strong arms, drowning in her beauty. 'Do ya think the same about us?'

Breathless from the feelings he stirred in her, she could only smile ecstatically up at him in reply.

'I know we ain't had long to get acquainted, but I swear I fell in love with ya the first moment I set eyes on that beautiful face of yours.'

'Some people know in an instant when they've met the right person,' Amber said gently. 'They don't need much time.'

'We got all the time in the world

now,' Jake whispered huskily, feeling the softness of her fragrant skin against his hands. Cupping her delicate face in his possessive grasp, he brought his mouth down to place a lingering kiss on her rosy lips.

'I got somethin' important to tell ya,' he murmured, gazing down into her trusting topaz eyes. 'I don't want to be a manhunter no more. I've lost the taste for huntin'. I feel it's time for me to settle down, and I figgered I'd use my manhuntin' reward money to set us up with a ranch right here in Copperstone.'

'Are ya sure, Jake?' Amber wanted to believe her dream had come true.

'I've never been more sure of anythin' in my entire life.'

The strength of their embrace sealed their future together — but Jake had one last matter to deal with before he was finished with manhunting forever: Lorn Catlin had done him wrong; before he could settle into a new life, Jake had to right that wrong.

12

Jake Farr cast a dark shadow over the green and golden patchwork landscape, entwined with opalescent rivers that tapered off into the distance like veins of silver. Behind him was a majestic ridge of awe-inspiring Californian mountains, but Jake was looking ahead towards the south. That's where Mexico lay. So too, lay his destiny with Lorn Catlin.

Two trails led south. Kel Lobart was away scouting one of them, searching for any sign of Lorn. Jake had ridden quite a way along the second trail, grateful for the fast and powerful chestnut bay with its gleaming black mane and tail which was loaned to him for the journey by Corey and Chuck Garrett. He found sparse evidence that Lorn had passed there. Nevertheless, instinct told him this was the way the outlaw had headed. His gut was sure of it.

Morning was giving way to the fierce heat of day when Kel Lobart came riding up to him at the appointed spot where they'd agreed to meet up. 'No sign of Catlin taking the south-west trail,' he confirmed, dismouting from his palomino.

Jake gazed at the south-east trail which stretched off into the heat-hazed horizon. 'I've got a gut-feelin' he's taken the east road.'

'Ya got to know him pretty well,' Lobart commented shrewdly.

'An' I got to see life from an outlaw's point of view,' Jake disclosed, his voice pensive.

'How did it look from their side of the fence?' Kel enquired.

Jake mulled over his reply for a moment before giving a one word answer. 'Bleak.'

Kel nodded his understanding. 'Least we've got a choice. Once ya turn bad, there's no turnin' back except of course if the law grants ya amnesty.'

Amnesty? The thought of Lorn being granted a pardon for his crimes hadn't occurred to Jake. Maybe if he was given a second chance to start his life afresh, Lorn would be a changed man. 'Think the governor would grant Lorn amnesty?'

Lobart's keen grey eyes viewed Jake sceptically. 'Don't ya want to see that varmint dead and buried?'

Ruminating over his answer, Jake's feelings warred against each other. Part of him wanted blood revenge. Part of him wanted Lorn to make it safely over the border to Mexico. Despite everything, he really had believed, even if only for a short time, that they were brothers. Jake had no family of his own and, although he hadn't realized it at the time, Lorn was the brother he'd always hankered after. Except for the badness that was bred in him since he was a kid, Lorn possessed his own kind of strange loyalty. Secretly, Jake was loath to hunt down Lorn and kill him, and he'd have to kill him for sure. No way would Lorn let himself be caught to rot in jail.

Kel knew Jake well enough to stab a guess at what was running through his mind. It happened sometimes, especially when manhunters got to know their prey personally, that they often found it hard to do their duty. 'Remember when we first met four years ago?' Kel began. 'Turned out we was both hunting the same outlaw?'

'I remember,' Jake reflected on the twist of fate which had brought them together and resulted in the foundation of their continuing friendship.

'I got a confession to make,' Kel admitted. 'I let that outlaw escape when I had him cornered in Billings, Montana.'

Jake was surprised. 'I always wondered how he got away from you. Took me another month to finally catch up with him.'

'When it came right down to it, I

jest couldn't kill him. An' he told me it was the only way I was ever gonna take him in. Said he'd rather die quick than fester in a jailhouse for the rest of his days.'

'Ya should've told me. I wouldn't have shot him.'

Kel shrugged his broad shoulders. 'Didn't know ya well enough then.'

'So, what we really talkin' 'bout here?' Jake questioned.

Kel spoke frankly. 'I think ya got too close to Lorn Catlin, especially ya thinkin' he was yer brother. Won't be easy huntin' him now.'

'I appreciate your honesty, Kel, an' you're right. I'm undecided what to do. But I know Lorn can't be let free to continue robbin' and shootin' innocent folks.'

'What ya want to do, Jake?'

A strained expression seared across Jake's face. 'We gotta do what's right.'

'There's little hope of Catlin bein' granted an amnesty,' Lobart remarked realistically.

In his heart, Jake knew that amnesty wasn't an option. The Catlin gang were hated all the way from Montana to California. A heavy sigh escaped the tension in his firm lips. 'Let's go git him.'

The decision made, there would no no turning back. The hunt for Lorn Catlin was fast under way.

★ ★ ★

Lobart was an expert at following a trail. Claimed it was because he was part Comanche. Jake's skills were more attuned to reading the character of those he hunted and anticipating their every move. Considering their combined abilities, Lorn Catlin's days were numbered.

★ ★ ★

Lorn sensed he was being hunted. He knew Jake Farr would be out to get him, no doubt accompanied by

Kel Lobart. Evaluating the combined calibre of these formidable manhunters, he realized he had an arduous task ahead of him. His main tactic was to keep well ahead and hope for a miracle that they couldn't catch up.

Miracles were in short supply for Lorn. He'd made the mistake of taking a detour into the rough-cultured silver-mining town of Silvervale, to rest up a while. Arriving in the late afternoon, he'd stabled his black stallion in the livery, paying for it to be fed, watered and rested. Then he'd filled his saddle-bags with supplies from the general mercantile, and booked himself into the Star Gem hotel. After eating a hearty dinner, and avoiding getting drunk to keep his wits about him, he went up to his room, locking the door so as not to be disturbed.

Three of the town's predatory buzzards had been watching Lorn. They wondered what was in the bulging sack he never let out of his sight. Most men who passed through Silvervale enjoyed letting off steam in the saloon, but not Lorn. He was too quick for their liking, which made them suspicious, reckoning he'd something valuable to hide in that sack of his. Together, they decided to wait until he was asleep, then break into his room and rob him of whatever was so precious.

Lorn lay on top of his bed, thinking he didn't trust sleeping in a town like this. Strangers were prime targets for thieves and gunmen. Although he was a light sleeper, tonight he prepared himself to sleep with one eye open, and his revolvers tucked under the money-bag which he used as a pillow.

Just after midnight the furtive sound of a knife grinding his door open and the jangle of a spur woke Lorn from his slumber. His hands tightened on his revolvers. Whoever was entering the darkened room wouldn't leave alive.

'He's sleepin',' one of the buzzards estimated wrongly. 'The sack's under his head. Must have money in it.'

The two other buzzards agreed.

'Rip it out from under him,' the first one whispered, not willing to do it himself, even though all three of them were armed with Colts, drawn ready to kill if need be.

The second man approached Lorn stealthily.

Lorn listened to their every move, watching them with half-shut eyes that were well accustomed to the dark. Lorn had vision like a wildcat — and was ten times more vicious.

Waiting until the thief was inches from the bed, Lorn jumped up, guns blazing fire in the blackness. No match for Lorn, the three intruders fell wounded to the floor, not one of them scoring a bullet against him.

Leaving them writhing in their own blood, Lorn grabbed his money and his saddle-bags and made a quick exit. Gunfire was common in Silvervale. Nobody bothered rushing to the immediate rescue of the buzzards. This allowed Lorn time to collect his black stallion from the livery stables and be on his way.

★ ★ ★

The manhunters had followed Lorn's trail into Silvervale, arriving there at dawn the next day. It didn't take them long to discover that a stranger dressed in black, riding a black stallion and toting a canvas sack which seemed mighty important to him, had shot three men in his hotel room then ridden out during the night.

'Them fellers picked on the wrong man,' Jake smiled wryly.

'Maybe they'll think twice before robbin' anyone agin',' Lobart responded in kind. 'Trouble always seeks out trouble,' he added sagely.

'I'll be glad when this is over,' Jake told his friend honestly. 'I'm tired of all the lyin', cheatin' and killin'.'

Kel nodded in agreement. 'The quicker we find Catlin, the better.'

'I reckon Lorn will be back on his original trail by now,' Jake deduced.

'Yup,' Lobart agreed, taking out a map from his saddle-bag. 'If we take this route here,' he pointed to a specific reference on the map, 'we should be able to cut him off before he reaches Coyote Creek.'

'Let's go,' Jake declared, instinct telling him he was going to meet up with Lorn real soon.

Lorn rode along an arroyo, following its dried-out watercourse which his map indicated led to Coyote Creek. This was the best route through the mountainous terrain which eventually opened out on to the vast plain again. Although he figured the manhunters would be hot on his heels, he hadn't reckoned on them watching him approach from their vantage point on the rocky ridge above the arroyo.

'Wait 'till he gets closer before we make our move,' Jake suggested the best course of action.

Kel nodded. 'I'll mosey along a bit,

in case he decides to make a run for it.' Heeling his palomino forward, the horse's hoofs dislodged a pile of loose stones on the edge of the ridges which tumbled down into the arroyo, alerting Lorn of their presence.

Looking upwards, squinting against the brilliant sunshine, Lorn saw the manhunters. Urging his stallion into a hollow in the watercourse, the outlaw gained a temporary shield.

'There's nowhere left to run, Lorn,' Jake shouted, his voice echoing in the stone-dry air.

'I ain't givin' myself up, Jake,' Lorn responded with gritted determination.

Jake quickly dismounted and scrambled down the sun-bleached rocks into the arroyo, securing a safe place behind a boulder. Meanwhile, Kel remained up on the ridge, his rifle trained on Lorn's hollow hiding place.

'Ya know I cain't let ya walk away from this,' Jake issued a warning.

'Maybe I'll be the one to survive,' Lorn stated with bravado. 'I've been in tighter corners than this and lived to tell the tale.'

'I'm asking ya one last time to come out, or I'll be forced to come in there and git ya,' Jake threatened.

'Go to hell, Jake. I ain't givin' myself up to nobody!'

From above, a warning shot rang out from Lobart's rifle, reminding him there were two manhunters he had to beat.

Like lightning, Lorn jumped out from the hollow, emptying his revolvers in Lobart's direction, letting the bullets speak his mind.

Jake ducked down behind the boulder until Lorn's rage ceased.

One bullet hit its target, winging Lobart in the shoulder, causing him to drop his rifle, which slithered down into the arroyo.

With equal speed, Lorn then retreated into the hollow.

'Ya all right?' Jake called to Kel.

'Yep,' came the reply. 'Don't let him git away.'

'I'm coming in to git ya, Lorn,' Jake shouted adamantly. 'I don't want to kill ya, but I sure as hell will.'

'If you're coming in, I'm coming out, guns blazin',' Lorn retorted with deliberate arrogance.

'It doesn't have to end like this,' Jake voiced the ultimatum.

'I'll take my chances. Are ya willin' to take yours?' Lorn challenged.

In answer, Jake stepped from behind the boulder, the Smith and Wesson already in his hand. Simultaneously, Lorn emerged from the hollow, only one of his Colts drawn.

As their green eyes locked, the Smith and Wesson spoke first, roaring a bullet into Lorn's chest. Lorn dropped to the dirt, his Colt slipping from his weakening grip. He gazed up at Jake, a look of sorrowful surprise in the depths of his green eyes.

Jake kneeled down beside him. 'Why d'ya use only one revolver? Whyd'ya do that?' he pulled at the reveres of Lorn's long black coat, trying to shake the answer out of him.

'Figgered it made us even, Jake. One against one, like brothers should,' he spluttered, blood trickling from the corner of his mouth.

Jake swallowed the sadness which was nearly choking him. 'But we ain't brothers,' he stated quietly.

Lorn smiled in pain. 'Guess I was beginnin' to believe my own lies, that ya really was my brother.'

'In another life, ya could've been,' Jake murmured wistfully. 'Maybe if I'd known ya as a kid, I'd have kept ya on the straight and narrow.'

'Maybe in the next life, Brother,' Lorn whispered in his final breath.

Kel Lobart had managed to staunch the flow of blood from his shoulder wound and had made his way down to Jake.

'Ya did the right thing,' Lobart remarked. 'Lorn Catlin was a black heart.'

'We all got a bit of darkness in us,' Jake reasoned. 'Lorn just never had nobody to look up to as an example of how to git the balance right.'

* * *

A fiery gold and rose sunset streamed across the Californian sky, as Jake stood alone on the brow of the hill overlooking Copperstone . . . remembering . . . remembering everything that had happened to him since he first arrived here. Montana, his home state, seemed a lifetime away, somewhere far off in the distant misty horizon. He would never forget Montana, but he felt it was time to start afresh. No more manhunting. No more killing. In his heart he wanted to settle down with Amber, and build himself a ranch in Copperstone with his hard-earned money.

As for his friend, Kel Lobart, he took Lou-Lou back with him to Montana, saying this was the best reward any man could wish for.

Strangely, Jake's story ended as it

began, with the day going out in a blaze of glory.

In the twilight, his tall, lean frame cast a dark shadow over the land, but tomorrow, he had a bright new future with Amber to look forward to. A whole new beginning.

THE END

We do hope that you have enjoyed reading this large print book.

Did you know that all of our titles are available for purchase?

We publish a wide range of high quality large print books including:
Romances, Mysteries, Classics, General Fiction, Non Fiction and Westerns.

Special interest titles available in large print are:
The Little Oxford Dictionary Music Book, Song Book Hymn Book, Service Book

Also available from us courtesy of Oxford University Press:
Young Readers' Dictionary (large print edition) Young Readers' Thesaurus (large print edition)

For further information or a free brochure, please contact us at:
Ulverscroft Large Print Books Ltd., The Green, Bradgate Road, Anstey, Leicester, LE7 7FU, England. Tel: (00 44) **0116 236 4325 Fax:** (00 44) **0116 234 0205**

Other titles in the
Linford Western Library:

RENEGADE BLOOD

Johnny Mack Bride

Joe Gage was a drifter who'd never had a regular job until, in Dearman, Colorado, he found steady work and met a pretty girl. But he also fell foul of the feared Hunsen clan, a family of mad, murderous renegades who decided he was their enemy. Joe had two choices: give up his future and ride out of the territory, or fight against the 'Family from Hell'. He made his decision, but he was just one man against many.

RIO REPRISAL

Jake Douglas

Life had taken on a new meaning for Jordan and all he wanted was to be left alone, but it was not to be. Back home, there were only blackened ruins and Mandy had been taken by the feared Apache, Wolf Taker. The only men Jordan could turn to for help were the outlaws with whom he had once ridden, but their price was high and bloody. Nevertheless, Jordan was prepared to tear the entire southwest apart as long as he found Mandy.

DEATH MARCH IN MONTANA

Bill Foord

Held under armed guard in a Union prison camp, Captain Pat Quaid learns that the beautiful wife of the sadistic commandant wants her husband killed. She engineers the escape of Quaid and his young friend Billy Childs in exchange for Quaid's promise to turn hired gunman. He has reasons enough to carry out the promise, but he's never shot a man in cold blood. Can he do it for revenge, hatred or love?

A LAND TO DIE FOR

Tyler Hatch

There were two big ranches in the valley: Box T and Flag. Ben Tanner's Box T was the larger and he ran things his way. Wes Flag seemed content to play second fiddle to Tanner — until he married Shirley. But the trouble hit the valley and soon everyone was involved. Now it was all down to Tanner's loyal ramrod, Jesse McCord. He had to face some tough decisions if he was to bring peace to the troubled range — and come out alive.

THE SAN PEDRO RING

Elliot Conway

US Marshal Luther Killeen is working undercover as a Texan pistolero in Tucson to find proof that the San Pedro Ring, an Arizona trading and freighting business concern, is supplying arms to the bronco Apache in the territory. But the fat is truly in the fire when his real identity is discovered. Clelland Singer, the ruthless boss of the Ring, hires a professional killer, part-Sioux Louis Merlain, to hunt down Luther. Now it is a case of kill or be killed.

GOING STRAIGHT IN FRISBEE

Marshall Grover

Max and Newt were small-time thieves, a couple of unknowns, until the crazy accident that won them a reputation and a chance to reform. But going straight in a town like Frisbee was not so easy. Two tough Texans were wise to them and, when gold was discovered in that region, Frisbee boomed and a rogue-pack moved in to prey on prospectors. In the cold light of dawn, the no-accounts marched forth to die.